Another Way Home
A Garrett Storm Novel

C. Marten-Zerf

Anglo American Press

LONDON, UNITED KINGDOM

Once again –

For my wife, Polly and my

son, Axel

Your light chases the

shadows from my soul.

Romans 13:4 - *For he is the minister of God to thee for good. But if thou do that which is evil, be afraid; for he beareth not the sword in vain: for he is the minister of God, a revenger to execute wrath upon him that doeth evil.*

This is a novel…that means I made it up, however…many of the people mentioned do actually exist. You all know who you are. Some of the scenes and places have been deliberately changed, this was done for two reasons, firstly to protect the identity of some involved and secondly as a narrative tool. If you would like to discuss the reality then please drop me an email at zuffs@sky.com

The men strained under the weight of the wooden boxes as they loaded them into the backs of four, ten ton, lorries. It was difficult work, the moonless night was exceptionally dark and, for security reasons, they worked without torches. But even in the darkness it was still possible to make out the Cyrillic writing stenciled crudely on the side of each of the wooden boxes, some of it half covered by shipping labels stamped with the current date, November 1984.

Sipho Mabena walked slowly down the line of toiling men, giving encouragement when needed and helping carry where he saw fit. It was slow work and should have been done using a diesel-powered forklift truck, but that would have attracted attention and Sipho could not afford attention at this time. Later, when the moment was right, then he would leak word of the massive, forty-ton, arms cache to the press. And then the ANC would tremble with fear when they found out that the Zulu Self Protection Units were finally well armed enough to truly take the fight to the enemy.

The small group of sixteen men were tiring fast, as much from tension as from the physical exercise. Moving over three hundred 125kg cases, in the dark, whilst not making a sound and under constant fear of detection was taking its toll. The two container loads had been offloaded the day before from a Polish ship, the *Agnieszka* and the white man in charge of security for that section of the docks had been bribed to look the other way between the hours of midnight and four in the morning. The rest of the security personnel on the docks were Zulus, so no further bribes had been necessary.

The two men in front of Sipho stumbled and dropped one of the cases that fell to the concrete with a loud crash splitting the side open. Sipho immediately whipped off his long overcoat and spread it over the wooden case, cursing softly at the men who had dropped it. He brusquely ordered them to get another case and, while no one was looking, he carefully turned the broken crate on its side and then, straining under the weight, he carried it to his car and dumped it in the trunk. He removed his coat, shut the trunk and went back to supervise the rest of the unloading.

And, unseen by anyone, the broken crate with the Cyrillic stencils leaked out its contents of plain river sand into the closed boot of Sipho's car.

Freedom Mabena laughed out loud, throwing back his head as he did so, his white teeth sparkling in the noonday African sun. The group of three girls that he was walking with joined in, their laughter high-pitched and birdlike next to Freedom's bass roar.

He was a tall teenager, a little over six feet and, although muscular, had still not developed the gross muscle mass of a full-grown man. He wore his hair long and braided and his off-the-rack clothes fitted him like they were tailored. This was his third week at Wits university and he had never before had so much fun. Being the only son from a very traditional Zulu family meant that he had been brought up under a set of rules and mores that most Europeans would have thought of as pre-Victorian in its strictness. As a result, he was pushing his newfound liberty to the very limit. He knew that he would soon have to buckle down to his studies but he was determined to leave them until the last possible moment.

Liezl, a tall blonde Afrikaans girl, rested her hand on his shoulder as they walked, both as an outward show of affection and as a physical staking of her claim. The other two girls walked slightly behind the couple. Handmaidens to the queen. They were discussing the party that would be held in the student's union building that night. A toga party.

Over three hundred students dressed in little more than a bed sheet each.

A white Ford transit pulled up next to the group of teenagers and stopped. A tall white man with a cropped military style haircut, khaki shirt and trousers and olive-green special forces boots got out from the driver's seat.

He pointed at Freedom. 'Excuse me. Are you Freedom Mabena?'

Freedom nodded his affirmation.

The white man pulled open the sliding door of the van and two other similarly dressed men jumped out of the back.

They grabbed Freedom by his arms and dragged him violently towards the truck. But Freedom fought back hard; twisting free from their grip he launched a huge overhand right into his one attacker's face. The man went down, blood spraying from his shattered nose.

And then the massive boom of a handgun rent the air. The driver pointed the still smoking pistol at Freedom. 'Get in the back of the van, kaffir.'

Freedom hesitated, knowing that the longer he drew things out the more chance there was of either the police or campus security arriving.

The man with the gun smiled. 'I'm going to count to three. One...two,' he turned the muzzle of the weapon to face Liezl, who had not yet moved. Rooted to the spot by the sudden violence. 'Don't let me get to three.'

Freedom put his hands up and climbed into the back of the truck.

CHAPTER TWO

Sipho Mabena dry scrubbed his face with his hands in a vain attempt to drive away the feeling of utter exhaustion that threatened to overwhelm him.

It had been three days since his son, Freedom, had been kidnapped. Three days of police inefficiency and the general malaise of Africa. They had been three of the worst days of his life but things were starting to happen. Witnesses were being interviewed and suspects were being interrogated.

However, things were not going well.

In a country where police efficiency seemed to be directly related to either ones standing in government or the amount of disposable income one had, Sipho was very far down the list. He was a low-level government employee and he took home just enough money to live no more than a comfortable life.

But it had only been two hours since he had received the ransom message on his mobile phone. And that had changed everything. It had been short and to the point. Reveal to us the whereabouts of the forty-ton arms cache and we will let your son live. Refuse and he will die. No police involvement. You have two days.

After careful contemplation Sipho had gone through all of his options, discarding them as he went until, finally, there was only one left. And still he hesitated.

Then, his mind made up, he picked up the phone to his secretary.

'Gladys, I want you to track down the cell phone number of my brother-in-law, Petrus Dlamini.'

There was a quick intake of breath before she answered back. Hesitant. 'Are you sure, sir?'

'Yes,' confirmed Sipho. 'I have nowhere else to turn.'

The laird of the estate had insisted that Garrett take some leave. Garrett had refused. The laird had insisted.

'Go and spend some time in a city,' he had counseled. 'No lone treks into the mountains. No solitary fishing expeditions. See some bright lights. People. Crowds. React with humanity. It will do you good, my boy.'

And because Garrett respected the laird. And because he did not want to draw attention to himself. He packed a small case and he left. But the laird did not know what it would cost Garrett.

To most of the people in the Highlands that knew him, Garrett was simply the gamekeeper. He stood six feet tall with deep green eyes. His hair a dark mane that fell to his shoulders, not through fashion but rather through his lack of seeing a barber. A quiet, solitary man who lived alone. Polite and taciturn yet with a well concealed aura of physical violence about him. He ran the laird's estate well and had done so for the last five years.

But to those who knew him before, those who had fought alongside him, or against him, knew him as *Popobawa* or The Beast. It was a name that he had picked up while fighting in Sierra Leon in a war of attrition that had ultimately cost him his humanity. Disgusted with what he had become he had resigned his commission and fled the continent to hide in solace in the Highlands of Scotland. Except he could not hide from himself. And so he had learned, instead, to live with The Beast. To keep it caged inside him, bound with iron will and deliberation.

Then, at the end of last year, a friend had called him. She had needed his help and he had been her choice of weapon[*]. He had gone back to Africa. Back to the land of The Beast. Once there, *Popobawa* had been released again - to wreak a terrible retribution.

Then he had come back to the Highlands. And this time The Beast lurked closer to the surface. Now he had to live with its fetid breath on his cheek and its growl in his ear. A constant companion. A reminder of his own self-loathing.

But the laird had bid him to holiday and so he had.

***

Petrus leaned back in the wingback chair, drew, exhaled and watched the smoke rise to the ceiling. No one had spoken for a while and the silence had drawn out to an uncomfortable length. Taut. Unyielding. Eventually he spoke.

'You called me,' he said. 'And I came. Without asking and without delay. Now, you insult me.' He swept the room with his gaze. The group of men and women sitting around the living room flinched as if scalded; such was the power that radiated from the man who had just spoken.

A woman stood up. She kept her eyes cast respectfully down. Her hands were clutched in front of her. 'Brother. May I speak?'

Petrus seemed mollified by the woman's show of respect. As a Zulu female it was the correct way to speak to a man. Especially a man of Petrus' standing in the community.

He nodded. 'Speak, Zinzi, my younger sister.'

'Sipho's family meant no disrespect. We are all distraught over Freedom's kidnapping. All they were trying to say is they would appreciate it if you could help us and, at the same time, keep bloodshed to a minimum. We need help but we also need to ensure Freedom's safety.'

Petrus grunted in acknowledgment. 'You all act as though I am some sort of *tokoloshe* or demon, wading through blood in order to achieve anything. This is not true. Perhaps in the times of the troubles when we all fought against *apartheid*, but now...I am a man of peace.'

No one spoke for a while. A few cleared their throats as if to speak but then said nothing.

Zinzi continued. 'What about last year? You and that foreign white man?'

'Garrett,' interrupted Petrus. 'His name is Garrett.'

'Whatever his name is, brother, you and him started a war and it ended in the deaths of thousands.'

Petrus sniffed disdainfully. 'Hardly thousands. Barely even hundreds. Anyway, it was necessary.'

'Yes,' agreed Zinzi. 'It is always necessary. That is the problem.'

Petrus stood up abruptly. He stood six foot tall, his hair cropped close to his skull with only the faintest hint of gray. His jeans molded to his long muscular legs and his cotton shirt, open due to the heat, revealed ripped abdominals and a breadth of chest befitting a man who had fought with spear and shield for all of his life.

Every exposed area of flesh showed a scar of some sort. Cuts, abrasions, small puckered gunshot wounds and badly stitched blade-wounds. The body of a man that had been hacked from the solid rock by the gods of war. Scarred and weathered but unbeaten.

'Freedom is like a son to me,' he said, his voice a deep bass growl. 'And if I have to swim through rivers of blood and climb mountains of flesh to find him I shall do so. You,' he pointed at the people sitting around him. 'You, civilized people have called me, and then you attempt to place strictures upon me so that you can sooth your souls. It was not *us*, you can say. *We* told him not to kill. *We* warned him.' Petrus bent over and picked up a blanket wrapped object from next to the chair he had been sitting in. He unrolled the object and held it in front of him. Two foot of polished steel blade attached to a short hardwood staff. A Zulu assegai. 'This will show me the way.' Once more his gaze flayed the people in the room. 'You sicken me,' he said as he strode to the front door and opened it to leave. 'I will call you when I have found my nephew.'

***

Garrett didn't like cities. But for Edinburgh he'd make an exception. The stolid gray stone buildings built so close together that the narrow wynds could hardly fit two abreast. The cobbled streets of the

Old Town and the looming presence of the castle all came together to make a city that felt old without being decrepit, mysterious without being murky. Unyielding. Dependable.

He had simply been wandering the streets and wynds for the last hour, breathing the frigid air and absorbing the feel of the city. Looking for nothing in particular. Merely looking. Striving to find solitude in a city of almost half a million souls. Seeking the dark. Not because he spurned the light. Nor because he found any deep significance about being in the shadow. He sort the gloom because he knew that were the light did not go, neither did many people.

It was mid-November, the average temperature hovered just above freezing and it rained one day out of every three. However, rain and cold suited the city. The shine of moonlight off the wet walls and streets and the crispness in the air providing a further level of gravitas to the city's calm dignity. A palette of blue and granite painted with steady hand. A solidity of purpose. The beauty of austerity brought alive by centuries of history.

But even cities such as Edinburgh had their sinister side. For every successful ecosystem must have its bottom feeders.

They came from the shadows. A group of five or six men. Heavily tattooed. Sparsely dressed in spite of the temperature. Studs in noses and eyebrows. Ridges of scar tissue on their foreheads and across their knuckles. Hard wiry men made harder by their Spartan existence. Urban hyenas.

'Hey, mister. You lost?'

Garrett stopped walking and cursed himself under his breath for allowing himself to have been so inattentive.

'I asked if you were lost.'

Garrett said nothing. The pack drew closer. Crowding in. Their breath steaming in the air. Their odor rancid with sweat and sour wine and marijuana.

'You must be lost or what would you be doing in our street?'

Garrett moved to his right, putting his back against the wall. Only three sides to protect. He scanned the pack. No problem. Street fighters, head-butters and kickers. Not a pro amongst them.

'Go away,' he said, his voice low. Resigned. 'Go now before there's trouble.'

The pack leader giggled. High pitched. Nasal. At the same time Garrett heard the footsteps. Hurried and staccato. High heels. Voices. Breathless. Nervous. Two girls talking. American accents. Tourists. Lost in the dark side of the city. Not yet afraid but definitely anxious.

'Oh-ho,' said pack leader. 'This just got interesting.' He flicked his head. 'Angus, Rab. Go get the lassies.'

Two of the hyenas split from the pack. They ran to the girls and dragged them, squealing and kicking, to the leader.

'Don't do this,' warned Garrett. 'Let the girls go.' Inside him he felt the Beast batter at its bars. Grunting as it tried to force it's way free.

The leader pulled a knife from his jacket. He flicked it open with one hand. The blade gleamed in the moonlight. Four inches of serrated stainless-steel pain. He held the blade high and pointed it at Garrett. 'Time to learn some respect, boy.'

In the past ten years Garrett had fought in over seventeen different conflicts in both Africa and Europe. He had been shot four times. He had been cut over twenty times. He had killed more people than the last outbreak of bird flu. And he was still alive. The main reason that some combatants live while so many around them do not is ultimately down to one major factor. That factor is, reaction time. The slow die. Those who have no quantifiable time between thought and deed, live.

The Beast's reaction was instantaneous. He grabbed the leader's wrist with his left hand. Then he swiveled and brought his right fist up in a savage uppercut, connecting the hyena's elbow, shattering the joint and bending the arm back at an impossible right angle. He moved fluidly on to the next night crawler, grabbing him by his ears and dragging him into a vicious head butt. The man's nose disintegrated with a sound like a heel on gravel.

The soldier stepped over the now prostrate head butt victim and grasped the third assailant by the belt and collar. Garrett lifted him with ease. He held the man above his head for a moment and then used him as a bludgeon to strike down the fourth pack member. Angus and Rab, who had been holding the girls, disappeared into the night. Running from the nightmare that they had conjured up.

The two American girls stood together, quivering. Holding hands. And before Garrett could stop him, The Beast howled.

The girls turned and ran.

Garrett glanced at the four broken bodies around him. Three were unconscious. He didn't think that they were dead.

The leader was curled into the fetal position, his shattered arm cradled to his chest. Garrett lent down, grabbed the knife from next to him and flicked it into the storm drain.

Then he stood up and walked away.

As he turned the corner his cell phone rang, the strains of Henrik Wienlawskis violin concerto singing into the frigid night air. He looked at the screen but didn't recognize the number.

'Talk to me.'

'It's Petrus.'

'My friend,' answered Garrett, his voice full of genuine pleasure. 'What gives?'

'I've got a problem.' Petrus explained the situation to Garrett. He told him of the kidnapping, the frustration, the family's fear. And finally of the ransom demand.

'No problem,' responded Garrett. 'Give them whatever's left of the arms cache. Problem over.'

For a while white noise took over the conversation, vague echoes and static and a hint of breathing.

'There is no arms cache,' said Petrus. 'There never was.'

And he told Garrett why. 'It was back in nineteen eighty-four, our Self Protection Units had been formed and trained in an attempt to counter the threat of ANC violence. As you know, us Zulus in the IFP never seemed to be able to raise the vast amount of funds that the ANC could and we desperately needed weapons. We needed the ANC self-defense units to know that we had access to a large quantity of arms, a sort of mutually assured destruction policy.

'So, in conjunction with some friends from the States, we imported forty tons of building sand packaged into 125kg weapons boxes. We kept the truth of the deal a tight secret known to less than six people but allowed the knowledge of the alleged forty tones of arms to leak. It worked perfectly, even our own top officers and politicians believed that we had managed to bring in a huge cache of small arms. We used it as leverage during the peace talks, threatened to unleash our Impis and the weapons unless at least some of our demands were met.'

'Okay,' said Garrett. 'I'll leave tomorrow night, I need to get out of this place for a while, anyway, there have been...complications. I'll get to Joburg the next morning. Text me your address, I'll hire a car and come straight to you.'

'I'll hire a car,' said Petrus. 'Pick you up at the airport.'

'No, my friend. No worries, I'll pick up transport at the airport. And one more thing, Petrus, whatever you do don't tell anyone that the cache doesn't exist. It's the only thing keeping Freedom alive. When they contact Sipho again he must tell them that the arms cache has been split up into multiple small packages spread over the whole country for security reasons. Tell them that you need at least two weeks to get them all together.'

'They'll never agree to that.'

'They have to. We need time. Convince them, Petrus. For Freedom's sake, convince them.'

Garrett cut the call. He cursed himself under his breath once again. Once again, he had lost control. The fact that he was protecting himself, protecting other innocents was no excuse. But that was his way, and he found solace in his belief that the only true evil is committed by the man who will not take sides. The man without the courage to decide right from wrong. The man who mires himself in the morass of compromise. Giving and taking until there was nothing left.

Garrett had long before taken sides. He would fight against iniquity in all of its guises and, right or wrong, he would stay the course.

CHAPTER FOUR

Rough hands dragged Freedom to a chair and sat him down. He had been blindfolded, hands strapped behind his back with zip ties and gagged with a short length of duct tape. They had driven for a long time. It was hard for him to guess at how long. Four or five hours at least. The last hour or so over coarse dirt roads.

A brief flash of pain as they tore the duct tape off. Another flood of agony when they cut the zip ties, allowing blood to pump back into his dead hands.

Then they removed the blindfold.

He was sitting in a small, stark room. White walls, badly plastered, a boarded-up window. Steel frame single bed, gray wool blanket, no pillow. A small rug on the polished red-painted floor. Wooden chair. In the corner, a steel bucket and a roll of toilet paper.

In front of Freedom stood a man. Tall. Close cropped black hair. A long but well-maintained beard and moustache. Khaki shirt and trousers. Military boots. His eyes were deep set, hidden in shadow. A human Rorschach test. A purple scar traveled down the right side of his face, pulling his right eye and the right corner of his lips together. A constant sardonic grin. There was no one else in the room.

'Greetings, Freedom. My name is Pete Vermulen. You may call me mister Vermulen or Sir.'

'Fuck you.'

'That's not very polite, boy. Please, do not mistake my civility for weakness. Would you like some water?'

'Would you like to go and fuck yourself?'

Pete took a step forward and struck Freedom with a casual backhand. The blow lifted the young man out of his chair and smashed him against the wall. Then the big man picked Freedom up and deposited him back on the chair. 'Next time I will use a closed fist. Do you understand?'

Freedom nodded.

'Good. You will stay in this room; you will obey all instructions. Follow these simple rules and you will not be punished. I will send someone with food and water.'

Pete left the room, locking the door as he did. He strode down a corridor, through another door and into another small, simply furnished room. This one had a desk, four basic wooden chairs in front of it and a worn leather office chair behind. A ceiling mounted fan ticked away as it fought an ineffectual fight against the savage heat. A single window was latched wide open. There were no drapes.

The big man sat behind the desk, opened a draw, pulled out a box of cigarettes. Lit. Inhaled. The fan chased the smoke around the room, dissipating it but not getting rid of it. Pete drew again. Hard. The burning tobacco crackled and a red tip formed on the end of the cigarette. A tiny nicotine driven volcano.

Against the one wall of the room stood a gun rack. On it was an array of various weapons. Mainly hunting rifles of different caliber, also two Vektor

H5s and a few pump action shotguns. In a cupboard next to the rack there were a selection of semi-auto handguns. Predominantly 9mm but also a smattering of 45s and a few exotics. Some would consider this to be a veritable arsenal. Pete knew, however, that anyone who tried to go to war with bolt-action rifles and handguns invariably got their asses kicked.

And Pete was determined to go to war. Over the last few years, he had come to the conclusion that the only way that the white man could survive and flourish in Africa was to have his own homeland. An area of South Africa that would remain forever white. He had gathered around him a small group of like-minded individuals. Mainly young Afrikaners who longed for the old days. The days when the white man had been king in Africa. The days when the South Africa Defense Force had ruled the continent with an iron fist. The days before Mandela had been released and the white Afrikaner tribe had lost the war.

But to fight a war one needed weapons. Modern assault rifles, hand grenades, RPG's and landmines. Pete had a backer. A gray man who worked in the shadowy world of high finance. He had never met him; he didn't even know his name as he dealt only through an intermediary. But the man was sympathetic to Pete's cause and, as a result, finance was no problem. However, since 9/11 the American CIA had tightened up on all forms of gun running and it was now close to impossible to get one's hands on any quantity of decent weapons, no matter how much disposable income one had.

So, he had come up with this plan. The Inkatha arms cache was general knowledge to anyone who had worked in the South African secret service as

Pete had done and, although he did not expect the whole forty tons to be left, he knew that a large amount of it still would be.

He had a force of thirty-nine men with him. They all lived on his farm in the Karoo. Many miles from civilization. The farm, or camp as they referred to it, was run on military grounds. Ranks were issued and discipline was strict. Apart from his second in command all of the other men were too young to have fought in the South African bush war.

Pete had done this on purpose. Although he would have welcomed the experience and expertise of these older battle-hardened soldiers, he also knew that they were all damaged goods. Men who had fought a war for generations only to lose and be cast out with no form of therapy or counseling. As a result, your average ex-South African defense force soldier suffered from various degrees of posttraumatic stress disorder including anger issues, overwhelming guilt and self-destructive tendencies.

In short – broken men.

They could fight but they were totally unpredictable, paranoid and dangerous to all around them.

The younger men that had joined Pete also had problems, these mainly being the rashness of youth. Pete stood up, walked over to the open window, lent out and shouted.

'Kobus, Bakkies, *kom hier*, Come here.'

Then he went back to his chair and lit another cigarette while he waited. Within a minute someone knocked on the door.

'*Binne*, come in.'

Two young men marched in, leaving the door open behind them. They were both dressed in olive drab trousers, t-shirts and military boots. They stamped to attention and saluted in tandem.

'*Kommandant.*'

'At ease boys.' Pete studied the two men. Over six foot, blonde hair, blue eyes. Wide shoulders and narrow hips. Proper Afrikaans boys. Strong, respectful and willing.

'Kobus.'

'*Kommandant.*'

'What happened to your nose?'

'The kaffir hit me, sir.'

Pete walked over to Kobus. Stood close, studying his crushed nose. 'Looks like he did a good job.'

'Yes, sir.'

Pete's hand whipped up as he grabbed Kobus' ruined nose and squeezed hard. Kobus squealed in agony and he dropped to one knee. But Pete did not let go.

'You are a trained combat soldier and you let an amateur get the drop on you. You disgust me. Bread and water for three days and extra duties. Perhaps that will teach you to be more vigilant.'

Pete turned to Bakkies. 'I am told that you discharged your weapon during the abduction.'

'*Ja, Kommandant.* The situation was getting out of control. The kaffir wouldn't get into the car so I had to insist.'

'Three fully grown trained men couldn't control a teenager without using a weapon? What weapon did you use?'

'The Desert Eagle, sir. The 50 caliber.'

'Did you pick up the cartridge?'

'No, sir.'

'So, you unnecessarily discharged an exotic weapon in a built-up area and then neglected to retrieve the evidence. You are worse than this piece of shit. Put your hands behind your back.'

Bakkies did so.

Pete punched him in the nose, dropping him to the floor. 'There,' said the big Afrikaner. 'Now you look like twins. Fuck off and think about how to improve yourselves.'

The men stood to their feet, shaky but still adhering to discipline. They saluted and left the room.

Pete smiled. They were good boys. He had to be harsh on them. Hard but fair. In that way he could at least offer them a small chance of surviving the coming war.

CHAPTER FIVE

Garrett landed at Oliver Tambo airport in Johannesburg, South Africa at seven in the morning. He checked through, rented a cell phone from MTN, a Nissan X-trail 4 x 4 King cab pick-up from Budget and cashed ten thousand dollars into high denomination Rand notes.

Once he had found his RV he typed in Petrus' address to the satnav, connected his iPod to the in-car stereo and pulled out, the sounds of Johann Hummel pumping through the eight speakers.

The traffic was thick and slow, many of the traffic lights not working. Scores of motor vehicles looked like they shouldn't be allowed on the roads; smoke pouring from their exhausts, mirrors missing and tires visibly bald. It hadn't surprised Garrett when he had read that over forty people a day died on the South African roads. That figure added up to around fifteen thousand per year. If one extrapolated those figures to the USA it would mean over a quarter of a million deaths a year in America. As opposed to the fourteen thousand that it actually was.

It took a little over an hour and a half to get to the place Petrus was staying. It was a large house in an access-controlled area called Kelvin. Garrett buzzed the intercom at the gate. They opened and he crunched up the gravel driveway and parked in front of the huge dwelling.

The house had been built in a clumsy blend of Mediterranean, Mexican, African, Roman and fuck-you style of architecture.

As if the owner had placed a huge pile of cash on the builder's desk and said, build me as much house as that can get me, and make sure that everybody can see that I spent a shithouse full of money on it.

Garrett grabbed his small suitcase from the loading area of the RV, walked up to the front door and knocked. As he did so the door opened to reveal his friend.

'Petrus, good to see you.'

'*Isosha*,' greeted Petrus, using his Zulu nickname, Soldier. 'Still alive, I see.'

'Apparently so,' countered Garrett.

The two men nodded at each other, the depth of their friendship plain to see but their characters unable to express it. They hugged each other briefly and then Petrus led the way into the house.

It was completely empty. No furniture. No drapes or carpets or wall hangings. In the corner of the vast entrance hall were two, fold-up camp beds, a small wooden table, a battery powered lamp and a gas camping stove.

'The right bed's yours,' said the Zulu.

'What the hell is this place?'

'It's the house of a friend. I'm looking after it for him.'

'Where's all the furniture? Why the gas stove?'

'He hasn't moved in yet and the electricity hasn't been switched on.'

'Really,' said Garrett, his one eyebrow rose quizzically. 'Surely a friend would turn on the power for you?'

Petrus looked sheepish. 'Okay, maybe not so good a friend.'

'Maybe more like a stranger?'

Petrus laughed. 'Maybe.'

'As in, he doesn't know we're staying here?'

'Look, *Isosha*, he's a relative of mine; I didn't see any reason to bother him so I just moved in for a while. It's cheap and I make sure that no one squats here. Anyway, he's got too many properties.'

'So, you stole his house?'

Petrus laughed again. '*Ja*. Come sit. I've got some beer in the cooler box. We drink, smoke, talk shit for a while.'

'Before we do,' said Garrett. 'I'd like to see Manon.'

Garrett was talking about a friend of his. A sister that he had met during the war in Sierra Leone. A few months before Petrus and he had stopped a kidnapping ring that had been abducting children from sister Manon's orphanage, the Sunlight Children's Home. He was also totally and inappropriately in love with her.

Petrus shook his head. 'I am sorry, my friend. She is no longer here. The orphanages were closed down and she went back to Belgium to the monastery.'

Garrett did not speak for a while. Then he pulled a pack of Gauloise from his shirt pocket. Offered. Lit both.

'So, let's have a beer,' he said, eventually.

Petrus took two bottles of Castle lager out of the cooler box, opened them and handed one to Garrett. They touched bottles in a toast and drank deeply.

In the darkness The Beast snuffled in sorrow. No Manon.

CHAPTER SIX

Five men sat around the boardroom table. There seemed to be nothing exceptional about them. Of average height. Expensive suits. Manicured fingernails. Gold wristwatches. Slightly overweight.

Every one of them was a millionaire. By the end of the month every one of them would be a multi-millionaire.

As long as everything kept going to plan.

'Gentlemen,' said the man at the head of the table. 'Is everything still on track?'

There was a general murmur of agreement.

'Mister Gabhela,' continued the head. 'You are still shy of the agreed amount.'

Gabhela nodded. 'Only a little. It is taking me longer than expected to liquidate my assets.'

'A million dollars is not, just a little, mister Gabhela. A million dollars is actually quite a lot. When will the money be transferred?'

'Soon.'

'You realize, of course, that timing is everything with this operation? Without your full monetary input you are useless to us. Worse than useless.'

Despite the glacial air-conditioning Gabhela was starting to sweat. Small, oily beads ran down his face, mounted his small range of double chins and disappeared into his Turnbull and Asser shirt collar.

'Please, it's only a matter of days.'

'Forty-eight hours, mister Gabhela. Two days. Then we shall have to take steps.' The head smiled; teeth pulled back to expose Hollywood-white teeth. The expression looked alien on him. Uncomfortable. 'Please don't disappoint us, my friend. Not after we have all become so close.' The head leant back in his chair. 'Business concluded, gentlemen. Leave me now, I will be in touch.'

The four men stood up, bowed fractionally and left the room.

Manhattan Dengana pulled a tabletop humidor towards him, took out a Limitada Cohiba cigar, clipped off the end and lit it with a table lighter. The blue smoke swirled around the air-conditioned room. Lazy spirals of burning money. Manhattan remembered the days during the apartheid era when his entire family would not earn in one month what this single cigar cost. Hunger was an all-day feeling, interrupted for a few hours every night by the fitful sleep of exhaustion.

Manhattan had grown up in SOWETO, the son of a laborer father and a hospital cleaner mother. He had graduated from high school in the early seventies and then gone on to get an engineering degree from the University of Botswana. It was then that he joined *Umkhonto we Sizwe,* the ANC armed wing.

During the mid to late seventies he went into exile, undergoing military officers' training in the Soviet Union, where he specialized in military engineering.

He then returned to South Africa and had successfully fought against the SADF for some two years. However, eventually he was captured after a skirmish with the South African security forces and, along with five others, was charged and later convicted of terrorism and conspiracy to overthrow the government.

The judge sent him to the Robben Island maximum-security prison to serve a 15-year sentence. While imprisoned at Robben Island, he studied for a Doctorate in business administration via correspondence with the University of South Africa. Manhattan was released in June 1990 under the terms of the Groote Schuur Agreement between the National Party government and the African National Congress. He had spent eleven years in prison.

When he had first got out of prison he had gone into politics, less for political ideals and more for its use as a business tool.

Now, a mere thirteen years later, he was a multi-millionaire with a large stake in Lonmin Plc gold mines.

But soon he hoped to be amongst the richest men in Africa.

***

Garrett and Petrus had drunk one beer each and then decided to reminisce while on the road. Time was of the essence in tracking down Freedom and it was imperative that they started straight away.

They had determined that the best place to start was at the university where the teenager had been abducted. They drove down Empire Road and turned into the Men's Hall of Residence. Garrett pulled into a parking, following Petrus' directions.

'Here,' Petrus pointed. 'He stays in Men's Res. He was walking a girl home. She stays there, Jubilee Hall. The kidnappers took him here.'

The two men climbed out of the car. Although there was nothing to look at they walked around the area where the abduction had taken place.

Garrett bent down and examined a few small drops of blood. Already faded and light brown from the sun. 'Whose?'

'Not Freedom's. Apparently, he slugged one of them pretty good. Then they pulled a gun, fired in the air and gapped it with him.'

'Witnesses?'

'Lots. No help though. Three white men. A white RV. They put him in the back and drove off. No one remembered any license numbers or such.'

'The girl?'

'She lives there,' Petrus pointed at the Jubilee Hall.

'Let's see if she's there. Have a chat.'

They walked over to the high-rise hall of residence and went into the lobby. There was a desk with a receptionist and two security guards. Garrett hung back while Petrus chatted to the guards and then to the receptionist. He beckoned to Garrett.

'Her name's Liezl. They've phoned her and she's coming down. Let's take a seat there.' They went over to a cluster of seats at the far end of the reception area, sat and waited.

After ten minutes or so the elevator doors opened and a girl walked out. She was tall and blonde. Tight vest top, large breasts, short loose skirt and two-mile-long legs. Earrings, ethnic bead bangles and necklaces, a touch of mascara and pink lip-gloss. Small handbag slung over one shoulder.

She radiated an aura of wanton sexuality in the megawatt range.

Garrett raised an eyebrow and Petrus grinned in unconcealed appreciation.

Both of the men stood up as she approached. She held out her hand. Garrett shook it, her grasp firm, skin soft. Then she shook Petrus' hand. Held it for slightly longer than propriety dictated.

Petrus' smile grew even larger.

'*Goie more, kerels.*'

'Could you speak English, please?' asked Petrus. 'My friend isn't much of a linguist.'

'Sorry, I said, good morning, guys,' she smiled at Garrett. 'I'm Liezl. I believe you're here to talk about Freedom. Are you cops or something?'

'I'm Freedom's uncle. Petrus.'

'Freedom talked about you often. Funny, I thought that you'd be older.'

'I am,' replied Petrus. 'This is my friend, Garrett.'

'Tell us, Liezl, how did it happen?'

The blonde Afrikaans girl took them through the kidnapping, her telling of it succinct and without embellishment.

'And the men,' said Garrett. 'Can you describe them?'

'*Ja*, but it won't do any good. They were the classics, six-foot or so, short blonde hair, tanned, blue eyes, well built. Afrikaans boys.'

Garrett swore under his breath. 'Not much to go on.'

Liezl opened her bag and rummaged around for a bit. 'Here,' she offered something to Garrett. 'They left this.'

Garrett took the offering. It was a short, squat empty brass cartridge. He turned it over in his hand.

On the base was stamped IMI .50. It was a cartridge he didn't know. He handed it to Petrus.

'Seen this before?'

The Zulu studied it. 'No. It's huge. I've got a friend, has a small gun shop in the Fourways area. We can ask him.' He turned to Liezl. 'Why didn't you give this to the police?'

She shrugged. 'What's the point?'

Petrus smiled. 'True. Can we keep it?'

'Sure.'

The two men stood up. 'Thank you,' said Garrett.

Petrus winked at the girl. She watched them walk to the pick-up before she turned and went up to her room.

CHAPTER SEVEN

Kobus shifted his stance and switched his crutch from under his right armpit to his left. The old-fashioned wooden support had been modified with an additional length of wood dowel that had been wired to the end so that it fit under his arm. Normal crutches are not designed to be used by someone who is six foot seven tall.

He wore a pair of old gray trousers that were at least six inches short so his right ankle and lower calf showed bare to his single shoe. The shoe itself was in fairly good condition, save that the end had been cut off so it would fit the tall man's size seventeen foot. On his left side the lack of trouser length showed six inches of sweat-darkened mahogany, crudely fashioned to resemble a lower leg and foot. The prosthesis was not articulated, nor was it anatomically correct. It was simply a dead lump of wood where a living lower limb used to be.

The top half of his body was clothed in a poncho that had been fashioned out of a wool blanket with a hole cut in the middle. Under that he had a shirt that was as short as the trousers. In an attempt to retain some semblance of neatness he had trimmed his hair with a knife. Likewise, his beard. He had achieved a ragged, chopped look that would have cost a fortune in one of Johannesburg's top hair salons. But all that he was worried about was looking kempt enough so as not to frighten people away.

In his left hand he held a small, neatly written cardboard sign.

'Unemployed. Please help. Willing to work for food. God bless you all.'

It had been a tough day; the sun was a hammer of heat on his head and the glare off the tarmac seemed to scorch his very brain. Someone had given him a pack of cigarettes, Camel, expensive. He had gotten no offers of work but had garnered a handful of small change. But now rush hour was over. It was time to start the walk back to his shack. He folded his sign, tucked it into his waistband and started down the road.

Kobus lived on the very outskirts of Alexandra. This was unusual as Alex was traditionally a black township. The big man could have opted to live in a white squatter camp like Coronation Park or Sunshine Corner, or any one of another eighty white squatter camps in the area that held upwards of two hundred thousand disenfranchised white Afrikaners. But he would not.

Some twenty plus years ago Kobus had been a sergeant in the South African Defense Force Koevoet counter-insurgency unit. They had been renowned as one of the world's most efficient fighting forces with a kill ratio of over thirty-two to one. They had also been notorious for committing savage acts of cruelty on both enemy and civilians alike. And ultimately, regardless of their prowess, Kobus and his compatriots had lost the war. They had also lost their own humanity in the process.

As such, Kobus figured that he no longer deserved to have a people. Friends. Family. He had declared himself outcast and thus lived on the very fringes of an already peripheral society.

He had lost his lower left leg below the knee in the last days of the war and had been discharged along with thousands of other soldiers into a world that he was neither welcomed nor that he understood.

The state had provided him with a basic prosthesis, aluminum with a partly articulated ankle. That had long since worn out and he was refused a replacement. So, he had fashioned his own limb. It worked but it was painful if he walked or ran for any period of time.

But Kobus welcomed both the pain and the hardships. He welcomed every new day that the Lord saw fit to punish him for his past transgressions against humanity.

The only thing that he retained from his past life was his small military-issue bible. He read it every night until the light had faded and darkness bade him to sleep. Or to simply lie awake in the gloom.

He stopped at a local convenience store and brought a half loaf of bread and a pint of full cream milk. The shopkeeper gave him two cents to make up the cost.

After another twenty minutes of walking Kobus was close to his dwelling.

'Hey, *Mithi*,' shouted someone.

Kobus smiled and turned to face the caller. A small boy, perhaps nine years old. Tattered clothes and mismatching shoes held together with string.

'How are you, *Mithi?*' *Mithi* was short for *Indlulamithi*, the Zulu word for Giraffe. Literally translated it meant, as tall as the trees.

It was little Sifiso's nickname for the big man.

'I see you, *Udokotela*.'

Kobus called the small boy The Doctor, because he was forever looking after his sick mother. A woman of indeterminate age that was dying of some wasting disease. Kobus had met her a few times and was convinced that she had AIDS. He had said nothing to the small boy.

'How is your mother?'

Sifiso shook his head. 'Very sick, *Mithi*. She doesn't even talk.'

'When did she last eat?'

'A long time. I have not found food for two days now.'

Kobus handed his bread and milk over to the boy. 'Here, take this to her. Dip the bread in the milk so that she can swallow easily.'

Sifiso took the offering with two hands and bowed deeply. 'Thank you, *baba*, father.'

Kobus nodded and went on his way. His stomach grumbled in complaint. He too had not eaten for a couple of days. But he had some cigarettes. And water. He was not sick. He would survive...or not. That was up to the Lord.

***

Pete drove his men hard. Each of them ran carrying a full-sized car tire above his head. On each back a haversack with twenty house bricks in it. On each hip a full water bottle. They had arisen before the sun and by now had run for over five miles around the sunbaked parade ground.

Pete was pleased. He raised a whistle to his lips and blew. The men turned as one and ran back to form up in front of him.

'Drop them.' There was a crash of sound as the tires and backpacks hit the ground. 'Now drink.'

The big Afrikaner looked at his recruits with pride. There were more now. Their numbers had swelled to forty-three in the last couple of days. Their time was getting closer and, as such, their training regime grew tougher.

He let them stand easy for a while as he stood and thought. He had phoned Sipho Mabena at four o'clock that morning and asked him where the weapons were. Sipho had vacillated. He needed more time, he said. The weapons cache had been split up into multiple small lots and would take weeks to get back together.

Pete believed him. It made sense. Sipho asked for three weeks. Pete gave him three days.

And now it was time to provide the father with a little motivation. He walked amongst his recruits, studying them as he did so. He needed two of them. They must be the right type.

'Lappies.'

'*Kommandant.*'

'Step forward.'

The young Afrikaner broke rank. He stood six foot four, over two hundred pounds, cropped blond hair and eyes of Atlantic blue.

Pete continued through the ranks, eventually stopping at a clone of the first man that he had chosen. 'Stephanus.'

'*Kommandant.*'

'Front up. You two follow me.'

The three men went into the house and trooped down the corridor to Freedom's room. Pete unlocked the door and ushered the other two in.

Freedom had been lying on the single bed and he sat up as the men entered.

'Good morning, Freedom,' greeted Pete.

Freedom nodded.

'I had a talk to your father this morning. It appears that he is trying to help.' Pete took his cell phone out of his pocket. Flipped it open. 'Remarkable things these,' he said to Freedom. 'I remember, back in the 1980s, when the first cell phones came out. Huge. Like carrying around a house brick. Big aerial. More like a field radio than a phone. Barely fit for purpose.' He pushed a button. 'Now, cell phones can take photos, video, messages. Incredible really.'

He focused the phone onto Freedom and activated the video. 'Lappies, Stephanus, show Freedom's father that we are serious men.'

The two large Afrikaners reacted instantly. One picked Freedom up from the bed and the other punched him hard in the stomach. The black man folded over and dropped to the floor.

'No, no, no, gentlemen,' said Pete. 'The face. Make it messy, I want to ensure that our intentions are clearly understood.'

The video capacity lasted for three minutes. It was long enough. Pete waved the young recruits away, lifted Freedom's unconscious body from the floor and placed him on the bed in the recovery position. He checked his pulse and ensured that his airways were clear. He would live.

Pete scrolled down his contacts menu, selected a number and sent the video to Sipho Mabena.

Then he smiled. A job well done.

***

Little Sifiso sat next to his mother. The shack that they lived in was little more than a lean-to of wood and cardboard. A giant's card-house constructed with careless hands.

The boy took a tarnished tin mug, filled it halfway with milk and soaked a piece of bread in it. Then he squatted next to his mother.

'Here, mama. The big man gave us some food.' He pushed the wet bread against his mother's lips. 'Please eat, mama. Please.' He pushed harder. Milk ran down her chin and dripped on the raw soil floor. Precious white pearls that shattered and drained away.

Sifiso gave up and ate the bread himself. Then he curled up next to his mother and went to sleep.

She had been dead for two days now.

In the morning little Sifiso would try to feed her again.

CHAPTER EIGHT

Petrus pushed the doorbell. The electronic lock buzzed and clicked and the steel door swung open. Garrett and he walked in. The door closed automatically behind them and then the next door opened letting them into the shop.

The gun shop was small but well stocked. Lots of shotguns, high-end over and under sporting models, hunting rifles and scopes. Some bows and arrows. In the glass topped counter a small selection of handguns. Revolvers and semi-autos. Thousands of boxes of ammunitions in shelves behind the counter as well as a case of bladed weapons. The air-conditioning was set to arctic. The place smelled of gun oil and frost. Vaguely unpleasant.

Behind the counter sat a massively obese black man. He wore a dark green three-piece suit and a purple shirt and tie. His face was covered in a slight sheen of sweat despite the glacial air. Petrus and he stared at each other for a while. Eventually the large man spoke.

'What the fuck are you doing here?'

Petrus smiled. 'Hello, Gatsha. How are you, my friend?'

'I'm not your friend. Go away. If I'd known that it was you at the door, I wouldn't have let you in.'

Petrus laughed. 'Garrett, this is my good friend, Gatsha Mazibuko.'

'Stop saying that I am your friend, what's wrong with you?'

'Pay no attention to him,' Petrus told Garrett. 'We're like brothers, that's how close we are.'

Gatsha shook his head, jowls wobbled and sweat dripped. He held his hand out to Garrett who grasped it. The strength of the grip almost took the ex-soldier's breath away. It took a great effort of will not to rub his hand when it was delivered back to him in a slightly rumpled, shop-soiled condition.

'You look like a semi-intelligent person,' said Gatsha. 'What are you doing with this degenerate?'

Garrett shrugged. 'Someone has to take care of him.'

Gatsha chuckled. 'Well, Garrett, please don't assume this is some sort of good-natured banter Petrus and I have going in order to cover our deep friendship. It isn't. I can truly say that I can't stand the fucker. He's trouble. Big trouble. But I owe him my life and it sometimes seems as though my debt will never be repaid.' He shook his head again. 'Sometimes I wish that he had just let me die, then I wouldn't have to put up with his stupid requests. Anyway, Petrus, what do you want this time?'

Petrus took the cartridge shell from his pocket and laid it on the counter.

Gatsha picked it up and studied it. 'Desert Eagle 50 caliber Action Express.' He placed the shell back on the counter. 'I don't sell these. What do you want with it?'

'Where did it come from?' asked Petrus.

Gatsha picked it up again and peered closely at the base.

'Look,' he pointed. 'See the imprint? IMI. Israel Military Industries. This is an old cartridge. IMI stopped making these back in the 1980s. Speer took over after that. I think I know where this came from. There's a guy, goes by the name of Sakkie Rebonowitz. His father was a Cape colored, mother was a Jew. Real Israeli one. He goes by his mother's maiden name, says it's better for business. He's small time, deals drugs, ecstasy mainly, also pimps out girls. Real young ones. He brought in a batch of these Desert Eagles a few years ago. Couldn't sell them for a while because they're such an impractical piece of shit, good for hunting bears maybe, that's all. You need to visit him.'

Gatsha pulled a scrap of paper from a drawer and scribbled an address on it. Slid it across to Petrus. 'Here, it's in Hillbrow. Be careful, this is one bad motherfucker. Really slimy piece of work.'

Petrus pocketed the paper and the empty cartridge. 'Thanks, Gatsha. Now, I need a favor.'

'I just did you a favor.'

'Well, I need another one. A bigger one. We need some weapons.'

Gatsha shook his head. 'No ways. Fuck off. It's not like the old days anymore. Gone are the times when you could buy an AK on the street corner, the government have cracked down big-time on illegal weapons. It's a worldwide thing since 9-11. Anyway, since when did you start using guns? What happened to your steel?'

'The assegai is still my weapon of choice, but Garrett prefers a firearm. Also, he needs that.' Petrus pointed at a 22" long cold-steel made panga-machete hanging on the wall behind the counter.

Gatsha took it off the wall together with a matching cor-ex shoulder-sheath and handed it to Garrett. 'No problem. Here.'

Garrett took the steel. Stood for a while, his eyes closed as inside him the beast fought for ascendancy. The smell of the jungle, hot and wet. Blood. People screaming for mercy as the steel blade rose high. Finally. 'Thank you.'

'Try it on,' said Gatsha. 'Take you jacket off, loop it over your shoulder.'

Garrett did so. The panga rode comfortably under his left armpit, handle facing down and ready to draw. 'It's good. Comfortable. Thanks again.'

Gatsha threw another sheath at Petrus. 'Here, you savage. It'll fit that assegai of yours as well.'

Petrus removed his light denim jacket and strapped on the sheath. After a few adjustments it fitted as well as Garrett's panga.

'Nice, my friend, but now, come on, Gatsha,' said Petrus. 'Gun for the man. And don't give me that can't be done shit.'

Gatsha pulled his chair to one side, then squatted down, lifted the carpet and pulled open a steel trapdoor. He picked up a steel box and dumped it on the counter. Then he waddled to the door and pulled a blind down to prevent anyone seeing into the shop. He took a key from around his neck, opened the box and pushed it across to Garrett.

Inside were two rusty Taurus .38 specials. Six shot. There was also a large selection of various gun parts and barrels. Garrett started to pick parts out of the box, seemingly at random. Within minutes he had a pile in front of him. Within four minutes, he had a fully assembled Colt 45 model 1911.

'I'll take this.'

Gatsha laughed. 'Well, fuck me. I didn't even know I had one of those in there.'

'Ammunition?' asked Garrett.

'Sure. Ammo's no problem. No one keeps a good record of it. How much?'

'Two hundred rounds.' Garrett poked around in the box a bit more and then took out an extra magazine. 'I'll take this as well.'

Gatsha replaced the box under the floor, took four boxes of FMJ colt ammunition from the shelf and gave them to Garrett.

'Right, gentlemen. That will be three hundred Rands for the panga and let's say five thousand for the gun and ammo. I'll throw in the sheaths for free.'

'Sure,' said Petrus. 'I'll pay you next time. Now we need to get going. Goodbye, my friend.'

Gatsha sighed long and loud. A steam train leaving the station. 'Not your friend.'

'Whatever,' said Petrus.

The door buzzed and the two men left.

Gatsha pulled a white kerchief from his pocket and wiped the sweat from his face.

Until now, Petrus had always been the scariest person that he had ever met.

Until he had seen the look on Garrett's face when he had first held the machete. A deep-seated fury held in check by the slenderest of ties. Ferocity covered over with the thinnest of veneers. A savage beast tethered by strands of silk and conscience. A man to be feared.

He hoped that no harm came to Petrus. Because, whatever he said, he liked that boy.

Truly he did.

****

Kobus rose with the sun. He had a headache brought on by hunger. He drank his fill of water from a bucket that he kept in his shack, splashed himself awake and stepped out into the street.

Then he shook a cigarette from the packet that he had been given, took a book of matches from his pocket and lit up. He drew the smoke in slowly. Savoring the pleasure of such a luxury. The hit of unaccustomed nicotine left him slightly dizzy and he squatted down while he smoked the rest.

They approached him while he was still sitting down. Three of them. Late teens. Perhaps early twenties. Young men made hard by a life of little worth. Petty thieves. Bullies.

'What you doing here, white man?'

Kobus said nothing. But he prepared himself. Slow deep breaths. Concentrating on what little strength his starving body still had to offer. Letting years of training and violence flood through him. Because he had seen similar situations to this before. These men were bored. They were dangerous. And they were looking for a distraction from their own shitty lives. He had seen other men in the township being beaten to death for little more than an alleviation of boredom. No disagreement. No theft. Merely a bit of sport.

He stood up. Registered the momentary shock in their faces as he stood six feet and seven inches high. At least a foot taller than all of them. He also saw the dull sheen of a knife in the one *tsotsies* hand. And he knew that he was fighting for his life.

The big man unleashed a straight right at the leading aggressor. Three feet of bone, sinew and stripped-down muscle. A poetry of mechanical force. His fist struck the knife wielder on his nose. The nose disintegrated with a sound like a foot crunching on a gravel drive. The excess energy carried on through the nasal concha and into the adjacent zygomatic bones, smashing both his cheekbones and snapping off his two front teeth. He dropped like he had been headshot.

Kobus stepped over the fallen man and grabbed the second attacker by his ears. Then he arched his back and pulled the assailant into a vicious head butt. At the last moment the man tilted his head to the side. Kobus's forehead struck him just above his eye, smashing the sub-orbital bone and knocking his eye out of the socket. It dangled against his cheek like some obscene parasite. Feeding off the host's blood supply and giving naught in return.

The third attacker turned and ran.

Kobus stood still for a while. Chest heaving as he struggled to take in enough oxygen to fuel himself. Waves of nausea flooded through him as his adrenal glands pumped him full of adrenalin. Too much. Too late to use. The fallen assailants lay still on the ground. As still as death.

The big man picked up his crutch and staggered off. He needed to get to his spot. Find work. Or food. His vision wavered as he walked. Sound came and went. The fight had drained his last reserves of energy.

He kept moving.

Slowly.

Not enough energy left to fuel his basic autonomic movements.

He knew that he was dying.

He did not care.

CHAPTER NINE

Petrus swore.

'What?' Asked Garrett as he climbed into the pick-up.

The Zulu passed his cell phone to Garrett. 'Sipho just sent this. It's Freedom.'

Garrett looked at the screen. Sipho had forwarded the last few seconds of a video. A video of Freedom suffering the most appalling beating. He handed the phone back. 'At least we know that he's still alive.'

'Yes,' agreed Petrus in a shaking voice. 'But the men who did that are dead. All of them.'

Garrett leaned across, grasped his friend by the shoulder and nodded. 'All of them. Now let's go to Hillbrow, find this Sakkie and get some info from him. Do you know the way?'

Petrus pointed.

Garrett started the pick-up and drove, following his friend's monosyllabic directions.

'Turn here,' instructed Petrus. 'See the Lamunu hotel there? I know the guards. We'll park there and then walk to Nugget Street where Sakkie's offices are. If you leave the vehicle on the streets here it's gone for sure.'

Garrett pulled up to a boom-controlled access. The armed guard recognized Petrus, gave a quick wave and opened the boom. They parked in the first space they came to.

Petrus had a chat to the guard and then they left. The Zulu had his assegai in its shoulder-sheath. Garrett had his panga and, nestled in the small of his back, the old Colt 45.

Petrus took the lead, walking through the crowded street with a swagger and arrogance that drove through the throng like a sawfish through a shoal of sardines. Garrett followed in his wake. Alert. Pulse raised. The body readying itself for action. And in a city where violent action was a way of life the lesser predators slinked back into the shadows as the Alphas stalked by.

They stopped outside a huge concrete and steel high-rise.

'Up there,' said Petrus. 'Tenth floor.'

As he was talking a television set smashed onto the pavement not five feet away from them. Glass and electronic chips buzzed through the air like shrapnel. A young woman fell to the floor, a gash over her eye pouring blood.

'What the fuck was that?' Shouted Garrett.

'TV,' answered Petrus.

'I can see that. Why?'

The Zulu shrugged. 'They've probably got a new one. Getting rid of the old one.'

'By chucking it out of a thirty-story window?'

'Hey, man. It's Hillbrow,' said Petrus with a grin. 'Come on, let's go up.'

They entered through a glass door, remarkable for the simple fact that it was still intact. On the right-hand side of the reception lobby was a bank of three elevators. Petrus pushed the call button and they waited. After a minute or so one of the doors opened. The two men moved forward and then pulled back. In the corner of the cab was a pile of human feces filling the elevator with the most appalling stench.

'No ways,' said Petrus. 'Let's take the stairs.' They jogged up the ten flights, taking the steps two at a time. Neither was breathing hard when they got there.

'End of the corridor,' said Petrus. 'Number one-oh-seven.'

They walked down to the end of the corridor. The door was sheathed in iron sheet metal and had three Yale locks running down the side. There was a stainless-steel intercom on the wall next to the door. Garrett pressed the button. They heard an electronic squawk from inside the office. The intercom crackled into life.

'What?' Asked a voice.

'Here to see Sakkie Rebonowitz.'

'Fuck off.'

The intercom went quiet. Garrett pushed the button again.

'What?'

'Let us in.'

'No.'

'Come on Sakkie. We want to do business. We got your name from a mutual friend.'

'Who?'

'Let's talk inside, Sakkie.'

'Wait.'

There was a pause as they heard the locks been turned and bolts being slid back. The door opened slightly, still on a chain. A man with a face like a beaver peered through the gap. Garrett kicked the door as hard as he could. The chain shattered and beaver-face was thrown back into the room. Garrett and Petrus ran into the room and closed the door behind them. It locked automatically.

Before Sakkie could get up Petrus walked over to him and held out the 50 cal cartridge. 'Is this yours?'

'How the hell should I know?' Shouted Sakkie. 'What the fuck is wrong with you people? You broke my door.'

'Listen and look, Sakkie,' continued Petrus. 'I need to know who bought this off you.'

'Get out of my office.'

'Sakkie, you don't seem to appreciate that this is a life-threatening situation that you find yourself in. Now, answer my question.'

Sakkie stood up and walked over to his door. 'Look at what you've done. Now I'm gonna have to call a locksmith and you know how hard it is to get a locksmith to come to Hillbrow?'

Petrus pulled his assegai from its holster and held it up in front of Sakkie's face. 'Listen, you moron. Start telling us what we want to know or I'll use this.'

Sakkie stared at the spear for a while and then he shook his head. 'I'm very upset. I think that you should leave now.'

Petrus looked at Garrett, his face a picture of puzzlement. Garrett shrugged; he was also baffled. The two of them were used to causing instant fear in their opponents and now all that was happening was that they were being treated like a pair of naughty schoolboys who had broken the classroom door.

Garrett decided to try a different approach. 'Hey, Sakkie, we need some information and we're willing to pay for it.'

'How much?'

'How much do you want?'

'One hundred thousand Rands.'

Before Garrett could answer Petrus lost his patience. 'Oh, for fuck sakes,' he grabbed Sakkie by his collar, swung the assegai like a cleaver, and chopped the drug dealer's right ear off. It fell to the floor and lay there, small and pale. A mollusk without a shell. Or a large comma of flesh.

Sakkie immediately started to talk. 'I sold the Desert Eagles to a man who owns a private security company. He took the three that I had left and all of the ammo. Ten boxes. His name is Sampson Sabelo. Company is Doberman Security. Please don't chop my other ear off.'

'Where is the company?'

'Not sure.'

Petrus raised his assegai again.

'Wait, wait. Krugersdorp, not sure exactly but it's in Krugersdorp. It'll be in the phone book. There, on the desk. Take a look. Don't hurt me.'

Garrett went to the desk, flipped through the book until he found the number and address. He tore out the page and put it in his pocket.

'Oh, great. First you break my door now you vandalize my telephone directory. You guys are real assholes.'

Garrett turned to Sakkie. 'Shut up, little man.'

'What? Sorry, I can't hear you because some savage chopped my fucking ear off with a spear. Christ, I think that I might bleed to death.'

'You'll be fine,' said Garrett. 'Wrap a towel around your head and go to the hospital. Take the ear; maybe they can sew it back on. Come on, Petrus, let's go.'

The Zulu re-sheathed his weapon, opened the door and the two of them ran down the stairs. As they emerged from the building there was the sound of a shot and a car window next to them exploded into shards of glass. Garrett looked up. Sakkie was leaning out of the window with a hand-gun taking aim for another shot. But before he could pull the trigger the sidearm slipped from his grasp and fell to the pavement, breaking up as it hit the concrete.

'Oh, shit. Now I've lost my gun. I hate you guys. You're like the prince of fucking darkness. I hope you get AIDS and die. Assholes.'

Petrus started to laugh and, within seconds, both he and Garrett were doubled over with mirth. After almost a full minute they pulled themselves together.

'Man,' said Petrus. 'That Sakkie is one seriously weird dude. Come on, let's go.'

They took off at a fast walk.

CHAPTER TEN

Precious Marwala had been Manhattan Dengana's personal secretary for over four years. He was a good boss. He treated her with respect, he remembered her and her husband's birthdays and, although he demanded long hours and absolute dedication, he paid very well.

In return Precious was a superlative assistant. At times Manhattan had even commented to friends and associates that Precious seemed to be connected to him via a psychic link, such was her ability to foresee his demands.

As it happens, Precious had no claim to extra-sensory powers of any sort. But she was intuitive and quick thinking. Also, she had short-circuited the telephone intercom system so that she could listen in to all of Manhattan's calls and meetings. This is how she managed to predict his every need.

It was also how she had gained the information that was about to make her and her husband into a very wealthy couple.

Precious had not overheard all of the meetings that Manhattan had been involved in because many had been held after hours when she had been at home. But she had heard enough information to know what she had to do and when.

She knew that in the next two weeks the South African Rand was going to drop in value by at least forty percent, or four thousand points. She did not know why, but she had heard her boss assuring the people in the meeting that it would happen. Her eavesdropping had also educated her as to how she could use this information to her financial gain. Manhattan had discussed financial spread betting with his compatriots. He did not discuss numbers or figures, but he did not need to.

After discussing things with her husband, Precious had gone straight to their bank and taken out a short-term loan using their house as collateral. The bank had advanced them half a million Rands, or approximately fifty thousand American dollars. She had taken the cashier's check to Capital Spread Brokers International and put it all down as a ten percent deposit on a bet of $125 dollars a point that the Rand would drop 4000 points, or forty cents, in six weeks. If the Rand did as Manhattan predicted then she stood to make over One million Dollars profit.

Now she was at home sharing a well-deserved bottle of champagne with her husband.

Life was good.

Then the doorbell rang.

Precious opened the door. Outside stood two black men. Both were well dressed in dark suits, designer ties and highly polished shoes.

'Good evening, Mrs. Marwala. Sorry to bother you. I am Colonel Zuzani of the South African Police Service. This is Sergeant Fumba, my assistant.' The Colonel held up a laminated ID card. 'Could we please come inside? We won't take much time.'

Precious ushered the two policemen in.

'Colonel, would you like a drink?' Asked Precious. 'We have champagne open.'

The Colonel shook his head. 'No thank you Mrs. Marwala. I don't drink European liquor. I find that it sours the stomach, do you have any traditional beer by any chance?'

Precious shook her head.

Colonel Zuzani sighed. 'A pity. Such is life. More and more of us find ourselves drawn to the European ways of life with their sour alcohol, their anorexic women and their disrespectful children. Never mind. May we sit?'

The Colonel sat before Precious could answer. He greeted her husband with a nod. 'Mister Marwala.'

'Colonel.'

Sergeant Fumba stood to one side, hands behind his back. Expressionless. Silent.

'Now, Precious. Do you mind if I call you Precious?'

Precious shook her head.

'Good. Precious, this morning you deposited a half a million Rands with a company called Capital Spread Brokers International. True or false?'

'True,' replied Precious.

Colonel Zuzani smiled. 'Good. May I ask why?'

'I'm sorry, Colonel. I don't understand.'

'Why did you deposit such a large sum of money with a spread betting company? It is a very simple question, Mrs. Marwala. Please answer it.'

'My husband and I made an investment.'

The Colonel shook his head. 'No, Mrs. Marwala, you did not make an investment. You laid down a bet. What did you bet on?'

Precious stared to sweat. Fat drops rolled from her hairline and down her cheeks. Like a precursor to tears. 'We bet on the Rand losing value against the Dollar over the next six weeks.'

'Not very patriotic to bet against your own currency, Mrs. Marwala. Not very patriotic at all. And such a large sum of money. You must have been very sure that you would win.'

Precious said nothing.

'Mister Zuzani,' said Precious' husband.

'Colonel Zuzani,' shouted the Colonel. 'Colonel Zuzani, you fucking peasant. And I am not talking to you.' The Colonel stood up. 'Now, Precious, no lies, why so much money?'

Precious said nothing. But now real tears had joined the sweat. They slid down her face in shiny rivulets and dripped onto her white collar.

'I overheard mister Dengana. I'm sorry. I have done no harm.'

'No,' said the Colonel. 'I don't think that you have. Tell me, Precious, have you told anyone else about this?'

Precious shook her head.

'Remember, no lies. If I find out that you were lying to me, I shall come back. And next time I will not be so polite. Are you sure?'

Precious nodded.

'And you, peasant?' Colonel Zuzani asked the husband.

'No one. I promise.'

The Colonel smiled.

Sergeant Fumba smiled.

'No harm done,' said the Colonel. 'Just keep this all between us. No one else must know. Agreed?'

Precious nodded. 'Agreed.'

She smiled.

Sergeant Fumba pulled a silenced Heckler Koch USP from a shoulder holster and shot her in her right eye. He swiveled and shot her husband twice in the side of his head. Then he re-holstered the weapon. He did not bother to pick up his expelled cartridges.

'Nice shooting,' said the Colonel. Let's go. Mister Dengana will be pleased. I'll phone him from the car.'

As they were about to close the front door a small ginger kitten walked into the sitting room and mewled plaintively.

'Hey,' said Sergeant Fumba. 'Check out the cute kitty.' He walked back into the sitting room and picked it up.

'What the fuck are you doing?' asked Colonel Zuzani.

'Taking the kitty. We can't leave it here, it'll starve.'

'So?'

Fumba gave his superior a reproachful look. 'Please, Sir. We aren't savages.'

Zuzani sighed. 'All right, bring the fucking cat. Let's go now.'

Fumba smiled. 'I'm going to call him Heckler, after my gun.'

'Yeah,' said Zuzani. 'Whatever.'

***

And in his office in Sandton City, Manhattan Dengana was planning to do exactly what Precious had just done. Except he was spreading his bets over a worldwide total of two hundred different spread betting companies. Also, he was betting a sum of $250000 per point. He and his cartel had almost raised enough cash to put down the required ten percent deposit. Everything was going according to plan. In a few short weeks Manhattan was going to make a profit of over One Thousand Million Dollars.

CHAPTER ELEVEN

Doberman Security was located in a three-story building that took up a whole block in Krugersdorp. The entire building was painted a matt black and the company logo, a snarling Doberman, was painted in gold above all of the windows and doors. This was meant to look intimidating but the harsh African sun had done its work and the faded emblems look less dog and more hobbit. Dull lines of faded paint sharing a joke with the peoples of middle earth.

Garrett and Petrus decided that they would take the polite approach to garnering information from the owner, mister Sampson Sabelo. This was mainly due to the fact that mister Sabelo was sitting in a building that was full of heavily armed employees. It was also due to the fact that Petrus had heard of mister Sabelo before. And he had emphasized to Garrett that Sampson Sabelo was not a man that you treated with disrespect. In Petrus' own words, he was one loony-tunes son of a bitch with his own private army.

The two of them removed their weapons and slid them under the seats of the pick-up. They wanted their friendly intent to be obvious and anyway, it would have done little good taking a few iron-age weapons into the lion's den.

There were two armed guards at the entrance door. Both were young. Both were black. Both were kitted out in the very latest in urban combat wear. Spider tactical body armor, black shirts and trousers, black special forces boots, Heritage stealth pistols in the 40 cal round and Vektor CR-21 South African assault rifles. They were probably the most intimidating soldiers that Garrett had seen for a long while.

Petrus, however, was unimpressed.

'Shit, these boys are so pretty. I think that I'm getting turned on,' he whispered to Garrett. 'Look at all their beautiful toys.'

The guards opened the double doors and ushered Garrett and Petrus into the lobby. Petrus batted his eyes at them as they walked in.

'Cut it out, Petrus,' said Garrett. 'Stop looking for trouble. Remember, polite.'

Petrus grimaced. 'Polite never works.'

'Let's try it. You never know.'

The black and gold theme continued inside the building. Charcoal carpets, dark gray walls with gold Doberman logos. Black leather chairs, smoked glass reception desk with gold trim. Funeral home kitsch.

The receptionist sat behind the desk. Black telephone with a multitude of lights and extra buttons, black computer and black Rolodex. Her hair was teased out into a huge 1970s afro. Red dress, matching red lipstick, dark blue eye shadow. Skin the color of strong coffee with a drop of cream. She was stunning.

'Can I help you gentlemen?'

'Please,' said Garrett. 'We would like to see mister Sabelo.'

'Appointment?'

'No,' replied Garrett. 'But it is important. We only need a couple of minutes of his time.'

She picked up the phone and punched in a string of numbers. A quick and quiet conversation followed. She replaced the receiver.

'Down the corridor, gentlemen. The double doors at the end. Three minutes.'

Garrett nodded. 'Thank you.'

Petrus gave her a wink. She lifted her head and sniffed disdainfully.

The Zulu nudged Garrett as they walked down the corridor. 'I think she likes me.'

Garrett shook his head. 'I don't think so.'

Petrus chuckled. 'Yeah, she does. I can see.'

Garrett knocked on the double doors and then pushed them open, not waiting for a reply. They walked into the office and Petrus closed the doors behind him.

Unlike the rest of the building, mister Sabelo's office was decorated with impeccable taste. A harmonious blend of traditional African and old European. Woven grass floor coverings, carved Teak wood desk. Hand stitched buffalo leather wingbacks. Vibrant African art on the walls. In the corner, a Sapele wood table with an array of cut crystal decanters. No gold. No Dobermans. An executive office. Apart from the Vektor CR-21 assault rifle leaning against the wall behind the desk.

Sampson Sabelo did not stand up.

'You have two minutes, gentlemen. Don't bother to sit.'

'Your receptionist said three,' answered Garrett.

'She lied. Talk.'

Garrett took the 50 cal cartridge out of his pocket and placed it on the desk. Sabelo didn't even look at it. He continued to stare straight at Garrett. The silence stretched out.

'One minute.'

'This cartridge came from a Desert Eagle that was used in a kidnapping a few days ago. We have been told that this selfsame cartridge came from a batch that was sold to you by Sakkie Rebonowitz.'

Sabelo shook his head. 'No.'

'Sakkie says differently.'

'He's lying.'

'First your receptionist and now Sakkie. A lot of lying going on.'

Sabelo nodded in agreement. 'Yes. It's a very sad state of affairs. Personally, I blame MTV. Your time is up. Goodbye.'

'Please mister Sabelo, this is important.'

'Leave.'

'At least look at the cartridge,' said Garrett.

Sabelo picked up his telephone. 'Stacy, send someone to show my visitors out. Now.'

Before he could replace the receiver Garrett, knowing that they had only seconds of face time left, leant over the desk, pulled the receiver from Sabelo's hand and smashed it against the side of his head. Blood flowed from his crushed ear.

'Where is the boy?' shouted Garrett. He grabbed Sabelo by the throat and pulled him across the desk. 'Where are you keeping Freedom?'

The double doors burst open and a crowd of armed men ran in. Five of them piled onto Petrus, forcing him to the ground, beating him viciously. Six attacked Garrett, striking him with boots and rifle butts. He went down under a rain of blows and curled up into a ball, absorbing the punishment.

After a minute or so the beatings stopped. The two friends were dragged down the corridor, through the reception and into the street where they were unceremoniously dumped onto the side-walk.

Garrett lay still for a while. Then he fumbled in his jacket pocket. Found a pack. Took a cigarette out, placed it between bleeding lips. Next his Zippo. Flicked a flame. Lit. Inhaled.

Petrus groaned. 'What happened to polite?'

'The guy's a dick head. Lost patience.'

'So did you get the number?' Asked Petrus.

'What number?'

'The number of the bus that ran over me. Shit, man. I'm broken. Those youngsters sure know how to kick a man when he's down.'

Garrett finished his cigarette and pulled him-self into a sitting position. Then he stood up. Slow. Painful. He held out his hand. Petrus grabbed it and heaved himself off the ground. His face was covered in blood from a deep gash above his eyebrow.

They walked slowly to the pick-up and got in. Garrett started up and pulled out onto the road.

'So,' said Petrus. 'What now?'

'How late do you reckon Sampson works?'

'Late,' said Petrus. 'I've heard tell that he often sleeps there. They've got sleeping quarters. Secu-rity is a twenty-four-hour thing.'

'No more polite,' answered Garrett. 'We go back to your stolen house, clean up, eat, wait until nine o'clock or so and then go back and demand some answers.'

'Won't be easy.'

'It never is.'

Garrett stopped at a set of traffic lights. A tall man stood on the side of the road. In his hands a small, neatly written sign asking for work. Garrett glanced at the man. Their eyes met. And the tall beg-gar keeled slowly over, banged into the driver's door and fell to the tarmac. Garrett put the hand-brake on and opened the door. The tall man lay crumpled on the ground. His face was shroud-pale. Limbs slack. Lifeless.

'Petrus, give me a hand.'

Petrus climbed out and the two of them man-handled the tall stranger into the back of the double cab. They had to bend his knees to fit him in.

Then they got back in and continued on their way home.

'So,' said Petrus. 'What's with the big stray?'

Garrett shrugged. 'Don't know. He's sick.'

'So?'

'I don't know. His eyes. Something.' He shrugged again.

'Cool,' said Petrus. 'Not a problem. Any other beggars that you want to pick up and take home you just tell me.'

'Fuck off.'

Petrus laughed.

***

Pete unrolled the papers onto his desk. He was alone in his study. The furniture reflected its owner in all ways. Solid African hardwoods and roughly stitched leather. Scarred from age and abuse. No art. No carpets. Bare light bulbs.

The map and its supporting documents had been dropped off by a middle-aged white man in a BMW. Pete had met him a number of times. He was the link between Pete's sympathetic backers and himself. They never spoke much; he knew that his name was Isaac Peterson but no more than that. He had his cell phone number if he needed to contact him and, the few times that he had, Isaac responded promptly and with efficiency. He had delivered the package and left.

The map was drawn to a 1:100 scale. Almost an architect's drawing. Pathways, windows, doorways. Electric fences, guardhouses, sentry posts.

There was also a pile of detailed photographs, both aerial and from street level, as well as a typed itinerary. The photos were instantly recognizable to anyone who had lived in South Africa for any length of time.

The photos were of the Union Buildings in Tshwane.

The South African seat of government.

And the president's official office.

Pete's plan was relatively simple. He knew, better than most, that it would be impossible to launch a successful coup with only forty men. Even with the coming arms cache. He knew that, even though the current South African National Defense Force was a mere diseased cousin of what it used to be, it still had over ten thousand soldiers under arms. No one could beat odds of 250 to 1.

But forty well-trained, well-armed men would be sufficient to take and to hold the union buildings. Or at least a portion of the buildings. The portion that contained the president of South Africa.

And then Pete would be in the position to make a few demands.

Demands that would have to be listened to.

And after that he would have ten tons of weapons to arm his people with. His new followers. The citizens of his new nation.

arrett poured a carton of orange juice into a large glass. Then he added half a bottle of honey and stirred until the honey had dissolved. He carried the mixture over to the tall man. The stranger was awake. Lying on one of the camp beds, swaddled in a sleeping bag. His eyes followed Garrett as he walked. He said nothing.

Garrett squatted down and held the glass to the man's lips. 'Here, drink slowly.'

After he had consumed half Garrett took the glass away and waited. A minute or so later he fed him the rest of the mixture. The man coughed a little but he kept the drink down. It was a good sign.

He held his hand out to Garrett. Shook.

'Kobus,' the tall man rasped. 'Kobus Vortser.'

'Garrett. This is Petrus.'

Kobus looked at Petrus. 'The Zulu prince. I have heard of you.'

'Nah,' denied Petrus. 'Must be some other Zulu prince that lives around here.'

'How did I get here?'

'You passed out. We picked you up and brought you here,' answered Garrett. 'I've seen this before. Uganda, mid 1980s. We were tasked with hunting down the warlord Joseph Kony. Teamed up with some American special forces. Came across a camp where Kony had imprisoned an entire village and was starving them to death. The villagers were in bamboo cages. No food or water. But they hadn't given up; they were throwing themselves against the bars. Literally trying to smash their way free. The lack of food combined with the huge expenditure of energy killed them quicker than usual. Your body simply doesn't have enough energy to stay alive.'

Garrett sat for a while. Silent. Visions of death filled his mind. Women. Children. Caged like animals. Torn flesh. Broken teeth from trying to gnaw through the bamboo bars. The dead and the dying rammed together. An Hieronymus Bosch painting of hell. He shook his head. Trying to physically displace the images.

'Anyway, Kobus. You should be all right. I'll make you another drink of juice and honey and then we'll try for some peanut butter sandwiches. Then sleep. Petrus and I will be going out later so don't you worry. R& R is what you need right now.'

Garrett mixed another drink. Kobus drank and then fell asleep almost immediately. His breathing strong and regular.

Garrett had stopped at the hardware store on the way home to buy a tube of superglue. He used this to glue the cut above Petrus' eye. Then they both showered and changed. Dark trousers and shirts. Loose dark jackets and combat boots. Weapons concealed by the coats.

'What's the plan?' Asked Petrus.

'No plan yet. We go, take a look. Find some way to sneak in. Smack Sampson around a bit until he tells us what's going on and then bug out.'

'Let's go.'

The two of them got into the pick-up and drove back towards the Doberman security offices. They stopped on the way there to fill up with gas. Petrus went into the convenience store and brought a bag of *koeksusters*, a sickly-sweet local confectionary, deep fried and dripping in syrup. He also bought a couple of industrial sized black coffees.

Garrett parked a block away from the offices and they sat in the vehicle and ate. Neither of them spoke. They simply waited. Comfortable in their silence. At nine o'clock Garrett got out. Petrus followed.

They walked around the back of the building looking for a place to enter as the front was too well guarded. But all of the windows were barred. Garrett stood for a while. Scanning slowly from side to side. Top to bottom.

He pointed. 'There. That drain pipe. We go up there, onto the roof.'

'Then what?'

'Take a look,' said Garrett. 'Just above the roof-line. Looks like it could be some sort of skylight or vent or something.'

'Yeah,' answered Petrus. 'Or something.'

'Something is better than nothing. Let's go.'

The climb proved easy. The pipe was solid enough top support them and the metal had been painted with some sort of bitumen protective which, although sticky, provided a great grip.

Garrett had been correct about the skylight. A flat pyramid of smoked glass, four triangular sheets bound together with a rubber sealant. It was set into the ceiling of what appeared to be the boardroom. Long wooden table, loads of chairs.

After inspecting the skylights for alarms and finding none, Garrett used the blade of his machete to cut through the rubber mounting of the glass and then lever one of the glass sheets off.

The two of them peered in.

'Long drop,' said Petrus.

'You go first,' said Garrett.

'No way, I don't want to go first.'

'Okay, I'll go first.'

'Hold on,' said Petrus. 'I don't want to go second.' He turned his back to the opening and slid in, pausing for a few seconds as he hung off the lip by his fingers. Then he dropped. He hit the table hard and rolled, falling off the side into the chairs that went crashing to the floor.

They waited. One minute. Two. Three.

No one came. Garrett slid through the opening and dropped. He landed on his feet; knees flexed. Graceful.

'Show off,' said Petrus.

They went to the boardroom door. Waited. Listening. Garrett nodded and they opened it and slid out. They found themselves in a long dark corridor. Lots of doors. Cheap faux-brass plaques on each door. On each plaque a name or designation.

J. Simbada. P. Moleke. Stationary. Photocopier.

They walked down the corridor, away from the boardroom. Alert. One of the doors opened. A man stepped out. He was dressed in a suit. Holding a briefcase.

Garrett swung his machete hard, twisting it at the last moment so that the flat of the blade struck the man on the temple. He went down without a sound. The two men hurriedly dragged him back into his office.

Garrett checked his pulse. It was strong and steady. He pulled off the man's tie and used it to gag him. Then he pulled off the man's jacket and used the sleeves to bind his hands to his legs. Immobilizing him completely.

Satisfied, the two left the room, closing the door behind them.

At the end of the corridor another door. They went through. Yet another unlit corridor stretched both left and right.

'This fucking place is a maze,' whispered Petrus. 'Which way?'

'Left.'

'Why?'

'I always go left.'

'Okay.'

They went left.

Another door. Another corridor.

Garrett opened the next door carefully. Lights. Sound.

'We're close to the reception area,' he whispered. 'Softly now.'

They eased through the door and headed towards Sampson Sabelo's office. They pushed the double doors opened and strode in. Petrus closed them behind him and turned the lock.

Sabelo was standing in front of an open doorway at the side of the room. Garrett hadn't noticed the door before because it was artfully concealed in the wood paneling.

Garrett whipped out his Colt 45. 'Don't move, Sabelo. You move, you die. Understand?'

Sabelo stood still, said nothing.

'Say, yes I understand,' said Garrett.

'Yes, I understand.'

'Good.' Garrett kicked a wingback chair towards Sabelo. 'Sit. But sit on your hands. Lean right back. Petrus, what's in that room?'

The Zulu walked over to the open door and looked in. He whistled, low and long. 'It's a fucking armory. Wow, awesome. Hey, Garrett, check this out.'

'Soon,' said Garrett. 'Questions first. Where is the boy, Freedom?'

Sabelo said nothing.

'Petrus. This could take all night. Freedom is your nephew; you take care of it.'

The Zulu took his assegai from its holster and walked over to Sabelo. He stared at him for a few seconds and then leant forward and clasped his left hand over his mouth. At the same time, he stabbed the assegai into Sabelo's thigh, just above the knee. Sabelo screamed and bucked in the chair but no sound escaped Petrus' hand and the same pressure kept him in his seat. Petrus waited until the struggling stopped and then he took his hand away.

Sabelo glared at him with unfettered hatred. 'You are a dead man. Dead. You, your family, your friends. Dead.'

'Where is Freedom?' asked Petrus in a low, calm voice.

'It doesn't matter because he's also dead like you.'

Petrus clamped his hand over Sabelo's mouth again and stabbed him in the other thigh. This time he twisted the blade before he pulled it out.

Sabelo went apoplectic. But once again Petrus held him in place, his arm a steel restraining bar.

When Sabelo had calmed down Petrus removed his hand again. Then he leant close.

He held the assegai in front of Sabelo's eyes. The overhead lighting played along the cutting edges on both sides of the razor-sharp steel. The top three inches glowed a dull red as Sabelo's blood provided an inventive counterpoint to the silver. Life as art.

'Look at me, Sampson Sabelo. You have something to do with the kidnapping of my nephew. You will tell me or I will put this blade into your right eye. Then I will do the same to your left eye. Then I will cut off your nose and your ears. Look at me. Do you believe?'

Sabelo looked. And he saw a warrior. A man of his word. A man much like he was.

'Yes,' he said. 'I believe.'

'Then talk.'

'You will kill me anyway.'

'Maybe. But if you don't talk then I will make sure that you don't die. You shall live, blind and as ugly as a nightmare. Even pocket change hookers will spurn you. Your choice.'

'I had nothing to do with the kidnapping. But I think that I know who did. I was told to get some weapons for a group of white men. I brought some from Sakkie, some from a few other dealers. I was paid very well. I gave them to a man. He met me on the North Road outside Warden.'

'Why didn't you just give him some weapons from your armory here? You've got tons.'

Sabelo shook his head. 'No way. The police do spot checks all of the time. Every weapon has to be accounted for at all times. It's not like the old days.'

Okay, so who is this guy that you met?'

Sabelo smiled. In the same way that a shark pulls back its lips before an attack. 'He didn't give me his name. But I recognized him. Pete Vermulen.'

Petrus literally took a step back. 'What? The Prophet?'

'The very same.'

'What's the problem?' Asked Garrett. 'Who's this Pete guy?'

'He was a member of the secret service back in the day. Big apartheid guy. Religious nutcase. Thought that God and him were best mates and God wanted him to kill all people of color. They called him the Prophet. He is one scary son of a bitch.'

'So are we.'

Petrus shook his head. 'No. Not like this guy. Have you ever heard of the expression, there is always someone badder than you? Well, that is this guy. He is always the guy who is badder than anyone. Fuck. Why did it have to be him?'

Sabelo was still smiling. Petrus backhanded him across the face. 'Stop smiling you baboon.' Petrus looked at Garrett. 'So, should we kill him?'

Garrett shook his head.

Petrus reversed his grip on his assegai and hammered the butt into Sabelo's temple. The managing director of Doberman security slumped off the chair and lay sprawled on the floor.

'Come on, Garrett, let's help ourselves to some weapons here.'

'I thought that you didn't approve of western weapons,' said Garrett.

'Usually, I don't. But that was before I heard the Prophet was involved. Now I reckon that a little extra firepower couldn't hurt.'

The two of them wondered into the small armory. Along the one wall were racks of Vektor CR-21 South African assault rifles and below them racks of Heritage stealth pistols in the 40 cal round. At the back of the room were shelves of ammunition. Thousands of boxes. On the floor were piles of backpacks, body armor and helmets. Next to them were two metal boxes, black with white numbers stenciled on them.

On the opposite wall were shotguns. Neostead 2000s. Below them a few Armsel Protecta Bulldog auto shotguns, short ugly weapons. Like old fashioned Tommy guns on steroids, capable of firing twelve rounds of 12-gauge buckshot in under three seconds. Banned in the USA after being labeled a Destructive Device.

Petrus picked one up with a grin. 'I'm in love,' he said as he went to the far wall, grabbed a backpack and threw in a few boxes of 12-gauge ammo.

Garrett grabbed two Vextor-21 assault rifles, a handful of extra magazines and five hundred rounds of ammunition. He put the ammo into Petrus' backpack.

'Let's go.'

'Sure,' said Petrus. 'How?'

Garrett pointed at the black boxes. 'Open those boxes.'

Petrus opened both of them, flicking back the clasp and swinging the lids back. Each box contained ten, cylinder shaped grenades.

'What are these?' he asked.

'Those are C60s. Multiple detonation stun grenades. You pull the pin, chuck it into a room and you get three separate detonations at one-second intervals. Those are CS grenades. Tear gas.' Garrett slung his two assault rifles over his shoulder. 'Right, grab a couple of each and let's blow this place.'

Both of them put one of each grenade into their pockets and held one of each in either hand.

'We'll leave via the reception,' said Garrett. Two gas then two stun. Walk through, don't run. Open the front doors and same again. Then we run. Got it?'

Petrus nodded. They walked to the end of the corridor and Garrett pushed the door open a few inches. There was no receptionist but there were four fully armed men standing in the reception area. He could also see another three, standing outside on the pavement.

'Ready?'

'Ready.'

Both of them pulled the pins from the grenades. The gas grenades detonated with a low thump and then skittered around the floor, pouring out clouds of CS gas. The men in the reception area immediately doubled over in pain as the cyanocarbon got into their lungs and started to shut down their respiratory systems.

And then the two C60 stun grenades ignited. Six separate explosions in excess of 160 decibels. All four of the security guards fell to the floor.

Garrett and Petrus walked swiftly through the reception area, holding their breath as they did so. The CS gas started to burn their eyes, ears and nasal openings. As they walked, they pulled out the pins on the next grenades.

Garrett kicked the front doors open and the tear gas grenades sailed through followed closely by the stun grenades. As the last stun grenade exploded the two men sprinted out of the entrance and broke left. Arms pumping as they ran as fast as they could. At the end of the block, they broke left again and continued at top speed to the SUV.

They threw themselves in. Garrett fumbled for the key, started the engine and pulled off. Garrett wound down all of the windows in an attempt to clear some of the CS off them.

It took him twenty minutes to drive home and Petrus swore, non-stop, the entire way.

'Bloody, bastard bloody tear gas. I fucking hate it. Stupid, useless son of bitch rubbish.'

Garrett laughed. 'Take the pain. It doesn't last long.'

When they reached the house Petrus jumped from the car, opened the front door and ran upstairs to the shower, undressing as he went. He turned the cold on full bore and stood under the cascade of water until the burn went away. Garrett did the same in the other shower room.

Then they dressed and came back downstairs where they found Kobus sitting up, back against the wall. In front of him were the two CR-21 assault rifles, the extra magazines, the Protecta and all of the ammunition.

'Nice weapons,' he said.

Garrett nodded. 'Yep.'

Kobus pushed the Protecta forward. 'Here, I've loaded this one. Also filled the magazines on the rifles. Have you used these CR-21s before?'

Garrett shook his head. 'Never even heard of them before.'

'It's a standard 5.56mm 35 round rifle. It looks fancy but the insides are basically the same as the R4 rifle. Think AK47 and you've got it. Works well. Where did you get them?'

'Stole them.'

'From who?'

'Sampson Sabelo.'

'Doberman security?'

'Yep.'

Kobus raised an eyebrow. 'You choose your enemies well. You got some sort of death wish?'

Garrett grinned. 'Not yet. How you feeling?'

'Much better. I chowed all of your bread and peanut butter. Sorry. Also drank all the milk.'

'That's good. We'll get some more food in tomorrow morning. Right now, I need some sleep.'

Garrett spread a sleeping bag on the floor and lay down on top of it. Petrus took a camp bed and Kobus lay back down on the other bed. Garrett turned out the battery powered camp light. Within minutes all three men were asleep. A skill born from years of combat. Sleep when you can, eat when you can.

CHAPTER THIRTEEN

Colonel Zuzani had joined the South African Police Service when it had first changed from being a "Force" to a "Service" in 1995. Ranks had been changed from the apartheid military style ranks to the British civilian ranks and Zuzani had entered as a Senior Superintendent. This was his reward for having fought for freedom during the struggle. He had no prior police training, no procedural knowledge and very rudimentary reading and writing skills.

This lack, however, did not impede his career in any way at all because, from the very first day, Zuzani had done little or no police work whatsoever. He had, in fact, spent all of his time creating an internal force of corrupt policemen that answered directly to him and then he proceeded to carve a place for himself in Johannesburg's vast criminal underground. Basically, he was a mafia don with a badge.

In 2010 the government had decided to change the Police service back to the old apartheid era Police Force and had told all employees that they need to take the Force to heart. Government sanctioned "Shoot-to-kill" orders were given to all personal and the Police force changed to become a paramilitary force that operated with a brutality that hadn't even been seen in the dark days of apartheid.

Zuzani's rank was changed from the civilian Senior Superintendent to full Colonel and all were issued new uniforms at vast cost in a country where almost 60% were starving.

Once again, this made no difference to Zuzani, apart from the fact that he no longer had a rank that sounded more akin to a head teacher than a policeman.

It was at this time that he had taken on Sergeant Fumba as his assistant and second in command. Although Fumba was still officially a Sergeant there was not an officer in the Johannesburg metropolitan area who would disobey his command. In reality he was treated as a Colonel. Zuzani was treated by all as a Brigadier. In fact, the only person that Zuzani paid even a modicum of respect to was Manhattan Dengana. This was because even Zuzani knew that Dengana was a man that it paid to keep on the good side of. In return Dengana passed on a lot of highly profitable wet work and he also protected Zuzani from any political enemies. The relationship worked well for both parties.

Now Zuzani had almost fifty guns under him and direct control of a Casspir armored personal carrier and a Eurocopter MBB BO105 helicopter.

At the moment, he and sergeant Fumba were doing the rounds. The two of them sat in the back of the BMW 750iL. The ginger cat lay curled up on Sergeant Fumba's lap, sleeping. In the front was the driver, Constable Tommy Thambo. Five foot five high and almost as wide. Fanatically loyal and as dumb as a box of spanners. In the passenger sat Lucas Buyani. A direct opposite to Tommy. Six foot six, willowy, small round John Lennon glasses and a mind like a steel trap. None of them wore police uniform even though they were all officially part of the uniformed division. There were times when the uniform was necessary but, when doing the rounds, plain clothes were more suitable.

The rounds were done every Friday, starting early. Zuzani would visit all of his enterprises, staring with the taxi fleet that he controlled.

The colonel did not actually own any taxis, he merely charged a levy on all taxis driving in his particular area of influence. Those who did not pay were constantly harassed by traffic police or, if their disobedience lasted beyond this stage, they met with some sort of disabling accident. Broken arms were a favorite. Sometimes the loss of a few fingers as well. And Zuzani was not a greedy man. He did not believe in killing the goose that laid the golden eggs. The levies charged were small and affordable. Most people paid.

The middle part of the day was spent visiting illegal drinking halls and gambling dens. Again, the colonel owned no shares in any of these establishments. However, those who did not pay their small tax to him were the immediate recipients of a police raid. These raids would continue until payments were made.

His final stop would be at the only business that he did actually own. The Farady Hotel in Orange Grove. The Farady was tucked away in a small side street off the main road. A three story 1970s shoebox shaped block. An asphalt parking lot in the front. A small, glass-door reception area and eighteen en-suite rooms. A subtle sign above the entrance read, 'Farady Hotel & Gentlemen's Club.'

The hotel rarely had overnight guests. Rooms were rented by the hour. As was the company. In a city that was already saturated by low-rent prostitutes, the Farady did exceptionally well. This was for a number of reasons; firstly, it was never raided by the police. Secondly, they provided access to the highest quality recreational drugs at fair prices and, thirdly and most importantly, none of the girls were over fifteen years old, nor were they below the age of thirteen. Zuzani had found a niche market and he had exploited it to the full. The place was kept clean and the girls were not overused. Zuzani enforced a strict 'five-per-night' limit on all of them.

The day to day running of the hotel was conducted by a Nigerian called Bam-Bam Balogun. Bam-Bam did not know it but he was in big trouble. This was because he had mistakenly thought that he could outwit the colonel. He was wrong.

The long black BMW pulled into the hotel parking and the four men climbed out. Zuzani opened his own door. The cat stayed inside.

Tommy led the way and Lucas brought up the rear. Their eyes moved constantly. Scanning. Protecting.

As soon as they entered the lobby Bam-Bam scurried across the floor to greet them.

'Colonel. Howzit? Good to see you. Come through to the office.'

None of the men greeted Bam-Bam back; they simply followed him through the door to his office.

The office was not large, A desk, one chair behind it, two in front. On the side wall a small two-seater sofa. On the opposite wall a row of steel filing cabinets.

The colonel and the sergeant sat opposite the desk. Tommy and Lucas stood by the door.

'So, Bam-Bam,' said Zuzani. 'How are things going? Profitable, I hope.'

The Nigerian nodded. 'Very profitable, sir.' He opened a drawer in his desk and pulled out two large wads of cash. 'Here, sir. Each girl has signed for her separate transactions. There were no problems. The consumable takings are in this pile and the girl's money in this one.'

Sergeant Fumba took the two piles of cash and put them into his jacket pockets. They bulged out conspicuously but he didn't mind. He didn't bother to count the money. Bam-Bam would never be so stupid as to skim directly off the profits.

'So,' continued Zuzani. 'No problems you say?'

'None.'

'Good. Well done. You are running the business well. Perhaps I should look at giving you a raise.'

Bam-Bam shook his head. 'There is no need, sir. I am content and happy to work for you.'

Zuzani smiled. 'Of course there is no need, my friend. There is no need because you earn more than enough. Particularly when you factor in the thousands that you have stolen from me over the past three weeks.'

Bam-Bam shook his head. 'No way. Count the money. It's all there, I swear.'

Zuzani stood up. 'Mister Balogun, do you know why the Farady club is so successful?'

Bam-Bam said nothing. He could recognize a rhetorical question when he heard one.

'It is because we sell only the best merchandise, both the drugs and the girls. And, what is my strict rule about the girls?'

Bam-Bam hesitated. Not sure this time whether the question was rhetorical or not.

'Answer me, mister Balogun and do so quickly or I shall cut your lips off.'

'Keep the girls happy. No more than five customers a night.'

Zuzani smiled again. 'Very good. So then, mister Balogun. Bam-Bam. Could you tell me why you are whoring them out six, seven, eight times a night?'

'Never, colonel. Never.'

Zuzani beckoned to Bam-Bam. 'Come here.' The Nigerian walked around the desk to stand in front of the colonel. 'Now, Bam-Bam, you disappoint me. Not only have you disobeyed me but you have also kept all of that extra money. And on top of that, you insult my intelligence.'

Bam-Bam was shaking in fear. Sweat rolled down his face like he had just run a marathon. 'Please, sir, it was only for three weeks. I am sorry.' He dropped to his knees. 'Please don't kill me, sir. Please.'

Zuzani sighed. 'Get up, Bam-Bam. I'm not going to kill you. But you will have to pay me all of the money back, do you understand?'

Bam-Bam nodded, his face a picture of relief. 'I've got it. Upstairs. In a steel box under my bed.'

'Good. Also, obviously I am going to have to make an example of you. I can't have people think that they can steal from Colonel Zuzani and get away with it, can I?'

Bam-Bam looked puzzled. 'Yes, but you said that you wouldn't kill me.'

'I won't. Sergeant Fumba will.'

Bam-Bam let out an inhuman wail. 'No, please, my master. Please, I'm begging you.'

'Yes,' said Zuzani. 'You are. Fumba, put him in the car, take him to Hillbrow, somewhere public so that people can see. Then shoot him in both knees and both elbows. Wait there until he bleeds out. Make sure everybody knows why. Then come back and pick me up. I will be upstairs with the two new girls.'

Fumba nodded and dragged Bam-Bam out to the car. Tommy and Lucas followed.

Zuzani stood up and walked towards the stairs that led to the new girl's rooms. Already his erection was straining against the confines of his silk boxers.

He smiled.

Life was good.

CHAPTER FOURTEEN

Garrett was instantly awake. Kobus was squatting next to him, his hand on his shoulder. He held a finger to his lips and then pointed to the window.

'There's someone out there,' he whispered. 'Multiple uglies. Seven, maybe eight. Here.' He passed one of the assault rifles and an extra magazine to Garrett. Then he duck-walked across the room to Petrus, wooden leg dragging slightly, and tapped him on the shoulder. Petrus whipped upright, his assegai at Kobus' throat.

Kobus didn't move but he whispered urgently. 'They're outside. Lots of them.'

Petrus crawled out of his sleeping bag and leopard crawled over to the window. He raised his head up slowly, like a cat stalking a bird. Then he sank down and crawled back.

'Five out front. I would guess three or more behind.'

'Who are they?' Asked Kobus.

'Don't know for sure. But they're carrying Vektor rifles so I reckon that they're Sabelo's boys.'

'Shit,' said Garrett. 'How did they find us?'

'Who knows? Sabelo is very well connected. Probably every cop in Gauteng has been looking out for us. Maybe someone even followed us. So, what now?'

'Let's get upstairs. If it were me, I would heave a few stun grenades in here and then come through the windows shooting.'

Petrus grabbed the Protecta and a couple boxes of ammo and the three of them crawled to the stairs and shuffled up to the first floor.

'Okay, guys,' said Garrett. 'We all lie down here. Wait for them to strike, let them come and I'll tell you when we fire. If they chuck grenades in, close your eyes, cover your ears.'

The three men lay on the floor, weapons trained on the area below. The killing field.

The sound of smashing glass. Two grenades sailed into the middle of the sitting area. The three men squeezed their eyes shut and clamped their hands over their ears. They could see the bright flashes through their closed lids and the massive concussions thumped them in the chest like a mule's kick. There was a crackle of automatic gunfire as someone fired at the front door, shredding the hinges and throwing the door back into the house.

Five men sprinted in through the large front entrance. They were carrying Vector assault rifles equipped with red laser sights. The laser sights projected thin red beams of light that danced through the smoke. At once both surreal and menacing.

Garrett waited until all five were well inside and he opened up. So did Kobus and Petrus. Both Garrett and Kobus fired fast double taps, point and shoot.

Petrus, however, went at it in the same manner he fought with his assegai. With great energy. He simply pointed the Protecta in the general direction and pulled the trigger as fast as he could.

A standard self-defense shotgun round contains eight lead balls of shot that are roughly the same diameter as a .38 special revolver round, and they strike with a similar force. Petrus fired off twelve rounds in a little over two seconds. This means that the five men below were subject to ninety-six shots in less than three seconds. To put this into perspective, it was the same as sixteen New-York detectives drawing their standard issue .38 specials and all firing all their ammunition off at once into a tight group of assailants. The few shots that Garrett and Kobus added to the skirmish were pretty much superfluous.

From the time that the stun grenades exploded, to the time that the five intruders were literally torn apart, was seven seconds.

'Yes!' Shouted Petrus. 'Now that's what I'm talking about.'

'There'll be more around the back,' said Garrett as he ran down the stairs. 'Wait here, I'll deal with them.' He sprinted through the kitchen and, without pause, kicked open the back door and dived through. As he hit the ground, he rolled hard right and then leopard crawled forward.

Then he paused. Waited. Still. His ears were ringing from the indoor gunfire but his eyes were fine. It was dark so he let his eyes wander. Slow scan. Let the peripheral vision do the work. Rods at the sides of the retina instead of the color sensitive cones in the center.

The back garden was overgrown. Grass over two feet high. Bougainvillea bushes, thick with flowers. The heady smell of honeysuckle and Jasmine. Male crickets chirruped, competing for mates. Warning off other males. Garrett had read somewhere that the average population density of crickets was around one per every square three feet of grass. That would mean that there were around six hundred in the garden, half of which were male. It sounded as though there were six thousand.

Garrett waited. It was conceivable that all of the attackers had come through the front door but it was unlikely. Someone was out there.

Five slow minutes crawled by, stretched out by tension and darkness and silence. The small area of back garden became Garrett's entire existence. A tiny battlefield in the middle of third world suburbia.

Somewhere in the two thousand square feet of unmown lawn and unpruned flowers, death waited.

But Garrett had more patience. More discipline. A movement. Slight. A mere breath that was deeper than the one before. And suddenly a darker patch in the grass became apparent. Garrett reacted immediately. He rose up onto one knee, brought the rifle to his shoulder and double tapped. By the light of the muzzle-flash he saw the second person, perhaps six feet away. Another double tap.

Silence.

And then Petrus, shouting from the door. 'Hey, you gonna take all night to do this?'

Garrett stood up. 'Done.'

'About time.'

'Now what?' Asked Kobus.

'Now we had better get the hell out of here,' answered Petrus. 'One or two shots and there wouldn't be a problem. But this is a fairly up market suburb so full-on firefights aren't the norm. The cops will be here in force sometime fairly soon. Let's pack up, put the bodies in the back, get out. We'll dump them somewhere else. Might confuse the issue. The cops aren't looking for work so they'll do the bare minimum. No bodies, no real crime.'

'What about all of the blood?' Questioned Garrett.

Petrus grinned. 'They'll overlook that. Welcome to Africa, my man.' He laughed.

Kobus gathered up the bedding and weapons. Moving fast, his wooden leg thumping on the tiles as he walked.

Garrett and Petrus dragged the bodies outside and piled them on the back of the pick-up. Then they covered them with a tarp. Tied it down.

The two of them climbed into the cab and Garrett beckoned to Kobus. 'Come on, get in.'

The tall man shook his head. 'Sorry, my friend. I thank you for the food and the help. I owe you, big time. But I can't get involved in this. I just want to go back to my shack, read my bible. Check up on little Sifiso.'

'You sure?'

Kobus nodded.

'Here,' said Garrett as he pulled a wad of notes from his jacket. 'Take this.' He proffered a sheaf to Kobus.

The tall man shook his head.

'Take it,' urged Garrett. 'If not for yourself then for Sifiso.'

Kobus took the notes and nodded his thanks.

'Come on, Kobus,' said Petrus. 'Why won't you come? You wanna go be a beggar again? Why? I tell you, my friend, it's better to burn out than to fade away.'

Kobus smiled. 'Enough time for me to burn in hell, Petrus. An eternity.'

He turned and walked off into the night.

'Wow,' said Petrus. 'Depressing, isn't he? It's probably because he's so tall. Doesn't get enough blood to his brain.'

Garrett started the pick-up. 'Where to?'

Petrus pointed and Garrett drove. They wove through suburbs and across a highway. After twenty minutes Petrus pointed to a large set of floodlit iron gates.

'There, I know the guards.'

'What is it?'

'It's a private landfill site. Household rubbish, trash that sort of thing.'

Garrett drove up to the gate and Petrus jumped out. He approached the three guards at the gate and engaged them in conversation. Muted. Heads close together. The overhead lights threw their faces into deep shadow. Featureless. Mere ripples on midnight water.

They carried shotguns. Chinese HL12 copies of the Ithica 37. Cheap and unreliable. Garrett wondered why they needed them. Who would want to steal junk? But then this was Africa and one man's garbage was another man's meal.

Petrus walked back to the pick-up.

'Two thousand Rand.'

Garrett pulled a wad of notes from his jacket pocket. Stripped off twenty hundreds. Petrus took it over to the guards.

The large steel gates opened slowly. Motorized. Small motors geared down to provide the necessary torque. As they crawled open the downward shadows created from the floodlights writhed and squirmed. Tortured souls in the night protecting the gates to Hades.

Petrus beckoned and Garrett drove through. The gates churned closed behind him.

The Zulu prince walked ahead flanked on each side by two of the guards. They both wore long black greatcoats. In the African style they had them draped over their shoulders, the sleeves flapping loose beside them. Demon's wings. Both carried powerful Maglite flashlights that penetrated the surrounds like lances of translucent silver.

Smoke from small spontaneous fires drifted across the vista.

They walked through a shallow running stream of fetid water. Oil slicks reflected back the torchlight in a myriad of diseased colors. The river Styx, separating the world of the living from the world of the dead.

After another five minutes or so they took a sharp right turn off the track. Garrett followed. Then they waved him to a stop.

Petrus walked back to the pick-up. 'This is it. We chuck the bodies out. They'll bury them. End of problem.'

Garrett climbed out of the cab and went around to the back to help Petrus drag the bodies off the load bed and onto the garbage-strewn ground. Then they got back in, did a tight k-turn and drove back through the gates.

Behind them the guards stood still, their wings flapping lazily in the smoke and the dark and the filth. Their light-lances shortened as they stabbed at the earth.

The gate dragged open and they drove out. Delivered from the Abyss.

CHAPTER FIFTEEN

Even squatter camps have their class divisions. Bad areas, worse areas. And even worse areas.

Sifiso's tiny shack was in the very worst part of the very worst area. Next to the Jukskei River, wedged between two larger dwellings and perched precariously on the edge of the water. To call the Jukskei a river was to be euphemistic in the extreme. Open sewer would have been a far more accurate description. Filled with industrial waste, human excrement and rotting garbage, it was less a source of water and more a source of disease, illness and infection. In winter it froze and in summer it flooded.

But one thing about it remained constant no matter what the weather. And that one thing was the smell. The Jukskei River stank like the very carrier of filth that it was. A sickening stench. A physical presence. A playground bully.

But as Kobus stumped towards little Sifiso's shack he became aware of another odor. A smell that cut through all of the others. A smell that took him back in time. To the killing fields of Angola. The wastelands of South West Africa. The burning villages of Mozambique.

It was the smell of death.

He hurried to Sifiso's shack and pulled aside the sheet of plywood that formed the opening. It took a full two seconds for his eyes to adjust to the gloom.

In the corner sat Sifiso. Knees pulled up to his chest. Hands woven together around his knees. Eyes wide and staring. Trancelike.

In the other corner lay a body. It was covered in wild flowers. Hundreds. Thousands of them. Most were shriveled to nothingness. But there were still some live blooms. Tiny splashes of purple and silver and white amongst the gray and black of the body's putrefaction. The smell of the dying blooms in direct competition with the stench of physical corruption.

Kobus crouched into the shack and squatted down next to Sifiso. The boy turned his head to look at him.

'Hello, Big Man.'

'Hello, Sifiso.'

'My mama is dead.'

'Yes.'

They sat together for a while. Silent. Respectful.

Then Kobus said. 'We must go now. Come to my place. We will get some food.'

'What about mama?'

'After we have eaten, we will take care of mama.'

'Promise?'

'Yes, Sifiso. I promise.'

The two of them left the shack and walked to Kobus' dwelling.

Behind them the river continued to flow.

Sluggish. Filthy. Uncompromising.

CHAPTER SIXTEEN

Freedom finished his oat porridge and placed the empty bowl on the floor next to his bed. He was incapable of eating anything more substantial. The beating had knocked out his two top front teeth and loosened the bottom two. His lip had been savagely split and stitched up by Pete. The stitches clumsy but adequate. Another row of Frankenstein stitches ran across his forehead, closing the long cut above his brows. He was missing the bottom of his left ear.

Pete opened the door and walked in.

'How are you feeling?'

Freedom said nothing. Stared at the floor. Not even acknowledging the Afrikaner.

Pete sat down on the room's single chair, reversing it so that he lent forward against the back, legs straddled.

'Fair enough,' he said. 'I'd also be pissed. It was a necessary evil. It is not my habit to injure without reason. I find no pleasure in causing hurt and I despise people that do. To harm any of God's creatures for no other reason than one's own personal gratification is sick in the extreme. Random violence, bullying, hunting for trophies as opposed to the pot. Sick.'

Still Freedom said nothing.

'Here,' Pete held out his hand. Freedom looked. Four white pills.

'It's codeine,' said Pete. 'For the pain.'

The young Zulu shook his head.

'Don't be stupid, boy. Take them. I know that I would in your position. There is no shame in it.'

Pete held them out again. Freedom lent forward, half off his bed. Took them. Swallowed them dry.

'Drink some water, boy,' said Pete. 'You should always drink a full glass of water with pills. Helps the body to process the chemicals.'

Freedom filled a tin mug with water from a bottle next to his bed. He drank painfully. Water dribbled from his swollen lips, mixed with blood. Dropped pinkly to the floor.

'Don't call me boy.'

'You are a boy,' responded Pete.

'It's racist.'

Pete laughed. 'Get off your high horse, boy. If you look hard enough you can find racism everywhere. However, if it offends you, I shall call you man. Or Freedom.'

'And what do I call you?'

Pete studied the young man for a while before he spoke. 'You can call me mister Vermuelen. Or sir. Or Uncle.'

'I will call you *madota*, man.'

Pete nodded his approval.

'So, *madota*, what am I doing here?'

'You are a hostage.'

'But my father is not a rich man.'

'True. But he has knowledge. We are holding you in return for that knowledge.'

'No. My father knows little. He is just a man who goes to work and does his thing. Normal. Boring.'

'Past knowledge,' said Pete.

'How?'

'During the war. Your father was a soldier. He fought for Inkatha. High up the chain of command.'

Freedom shook his head. 'No. My father hates violence. He is a mouse.'

Pete laughed. 'Ah yes, the certainty of youth. You know nothing, Freedom.'

'I know what makes a man. My uncle is a man.'

'Oh yes, and who is your uncle?'

'Petrus Dlamini. And he will come for me.'

Pete's grin faded. He sighed. 'I have heard of him. I did not know that he was your uncle.'

'Few do. The family is ashamed of him. Scared of him. They deny him. But he will come for me. And all of this, all these people, they will count for nothing against him.'

'Yes,' said Pete. 'I think that you are right. From what I have heard of the man, he will come for you. And then we will kill him. Because we are many and he is one.'

'No,' said Freedom.

'Even if I was alone,' continued Pete. 'He would not prevail. I am too good at what I do. No one can get close to me.'

'Someone did,' disagreed Freedom. 'Gave you that scar.'

Pete touched the massive scar that ran down the side of his face. 'That was different.'

'How?'

'It was a friend.'

Freedom snorted. 'Not much of a friend.'

Pete shook his head. 'You know nothing. He was the very best of friends. The very best of men. Honorable. True. I loved him like a brother.'

'Where is he now? This brother of yours.'

'He is no longer here.'

'You killed him?'

'No. Never.'

'What was his name?'

'Leon. Leon Povall. He lived for Africa, but he went far away to fight in the wind and the rain and the cold.'

'And soon my uncle will come. And you too shall die.'

Pete stood up and walked to the door. He turned to face the young Zulu before he closed it behind him. His eyes glinted in the weak light. Not human. Like wet river pebbles. Dark. Dead.

'No, Freedom, he cannot kill me, for I died a long time ago. A long time ago.'

The door clicked shut.

CHAPTER SEVENTEEN

They slept in the front of the pick-up, about a hundred yards off the road in a copse of trees. Three hours of uncomfortable semi-rest spent on the very edge of sleep.

The sun rose at five o'clock, Garrett started the pick-up and headed for a truckers stop where they could clean up and get some breakfast. They both ordered something called a belly-buster breakfast and a pot of coffee. Eggs, beans, bacon, lamb chops, sausage, fried onions, mushrooms, hash browns, kidneys and piles of toast were laid before them and they set at it with a purpose.

Afterwards they went outside and sat on a bench. Garrett took out a pack of Gauloise plains. Offered. Petrus accepted. They lit and sat for a while in the still morning air. The smoke hung above them, creating gossamer patterns of lace and web.

'We need to find this character that's holding Freedom,' said Garrett.

Petrus exhaled through closed teeth, spreading the smoke into tiny tendrils. 'That will be easy, someone always knows where that madman is.' The Zulu stood up, stretched his back. 'Listen, my friend,' he continued. 'This Pete Vermulen, they call him "The Prophet". He's a bad dude. Seriously bad. Look, what I'm saying is, you don't need to come with me when I find him. I had no idea that he was involved and, frankly, I don't rate our odds against him.'

Garrett raised an eyebrow. 'Come on. No one is that bad.' And deep down The Beast growled. Sensing an adversary. Another alpha to fight.

'They say that he can't be killed. Many, many have tried. He has been shot over twenty-seven times. He died once and came back to life. He has killed hundreds of people. He is insane. I met him once, long ago, during the apartheid war. He is the only man that I have ever been truly scared of.'

Garrett shrugged. 'Whatever, I'm still going with you. We're a team. And anyway, if he's so bad then we'll simply find a way to sneak in and steal Freedom from him. Avoid confrontation.'

Petrus grinned. 'Thanks, my friend. Now, let me make a few calls and we'll track this motherfucker down.'

Garrett lit another cigarette while Petrus dialed out on his cell phone. He made six calls in the next ten minutes then pocketed the cell.

'Now we wait,' he said. 'Someone will phone with his whereabouts in the next hour or so.'

Garrett tossed away his cigarette butt. 'Should we have another breakfast?'

'Yep,' agreed Petrus. 'Why not?'

***

Kobus fashioned a litter from two branches and a length of frayed tarpaulin. Then he and Sifiso wrapped mama in an old blanket. After that the two of them dragged the body six miles to the nearest cemetery.

However, when they got there, they were turned away. To qualify for a pauper's burial, they were told that they needed a certified death certificate. They would also need financial position statements with affidavits from the SAPS to prove they could not afford to pay. Letters from the Department of Social Welfare and Development, relevant Ward Councilor and or the Church leader, confirming the poverty conditions being experienced.

So, they turned and started to drag the putrefying body back to the squatter camp. After two miles Kobus had to stop. His arms were burning from the effort and his stump was chaffed raw against his wooden prosthesis. He sat down next to the dirt road, sweat drying into patches of salt on his shirt. He had no idea what to do next. But he had promised Sifiso that they would take care of mama, so, somehow, he would.

He took out his cigarette packet and withdrew the last cigarette. Lit it and inhaled. The smoke helped to drive away the stench of the rotting body and he drew deeply.

Little Sifiso had pulled up some dry grass and was weaving a bracelet out of it. It was late afternoon by now, almost early evening, and the sun had drenched the skies in a wash of red and purple and gold. Flocks of Mossie Sparrows flitted through the dusk in groups one hundred strong. Flicking through the air and turning in synchronicity. A poetry of flashing wings and shining feathers.

A car approached them, coming from the direction of the city. A large luxury automobile. Traveling fast. Dust boiled around it and hung in the still air like a battleship laying down a smoke screen. The driver braked hard and it slew to a stop opposite them.

The back door opened and a man stepped out. Medium height. Dark suit, white shirt, red tie. Expensive. His skin shone as if polished. Sleek and well fed like a racehorse. He walked across the road towards them. Fine dust settled on his shoes, dulling the shine with red talc.

'Is that a body?' He asked.

Kobus said nothing.

'It's mama,' said Sifiso. 'She is dead. We were taking her to be buried but they sent us away.'

'Why?'

Kobus stood up and answered, explaining about the red tape, the hoops that needed to be jumped through. The stupidity of the whole thing.

'That's bullshit,' said the man. 'Did you try to bribe them?'

Kobus shook his head. 'No money.'

The man pulled out a money clip. Unfolded it and pulled off notes.

'Here,' he held it out to Kobus. The tall man took it, using both hands as a sign of respect. 'Give that to them,' continued the man. 'And tell them that colonel Zuzani orders them to accommodate you. And not in the pauper's section. Tell them that the colonel wants a cross above the grave. Tell them that the colonel will be checking up on them.' He shook his head. 'Fucking basterds, turning away a motherless child.'

He turned and walked back to his car. Got inside. The car accelerated away. Huge and expensive.

Kobus pocketed the money, picked up the litter and, like Sisyphus pushing his rock up the hill for all eternity, trudged back to the cemetery.

In the car sergeant Fumba stoked his cat and spoke. 'Hey, that was a nice thing that you did there, boss.'

Zuzani turned to look at him. 'Shut up, sergeant. And if that cat gets any fur on my suit, I swear to God that I will shoot it.'

CHAPTER EIGHTEEN

They had been driving for over four hours.

Petrus' contacts had informed him that the Prophet was living on a large farm in the Northern Cape. Near the town of Postmasburg. Almost five hundred miles by road.

Before they had set off, they had stopped in at an Internet café, printed off a selection of aerial views of the area courtesy of Google Earth and written down the latitude and longitude. Garrett had also visited a hiking shop and purchased a set of ordnance survey maps of the district and a pair of Nikon binoculars.

Neither the Google images nor the maps showed much. A farmhouse surrounded by a number of out-buildings in the middle of thousands of acres of nothing. But at least they could pick out where the tracks were as well as the lay of the land so that they could work out where hills and tree cover lay.

It was late afternoon by the time they made the district. They decided to leave the road and use the GPS facility on Petrus' cell phone to get as close to the farmhouse as possible without detection. Then they would recon the place and take it from there.

Garrett jammed the gears into 4WD and took the pick-up across country, describing a large arc that brought them in from the East side of the farmhouse via a gaggle of low hills and shallow valleys that he hoped would hide their approach.

After forty-five minutes of hard off-roading, they stopped the pick-up in a valley less than a mile from the homestead. They exited and walked up to the top of the hill in front of them, keeping low as they approached the crest so as to avoid being silhouetted against the lowering sun.

Garrett focused the binoculars on the homestead.

'One main building,' he murmured to Petrus. 'Bungalow. Looks like three or four rooms. Not large. Two barns. One very dilapidated, the other, fresh paint. Lots of people going in and out of the renovated barn. Looks to be a dormitory of sorts. Chow house, latrines.'

'Where do you think Freedom is?'

Garrett scanned the buildings again. 'There,' he said. 'Second window from the front door. On the right. It's boarded up. That would be my guess.'

'Any ideas?' Asked the Zulu.

'I'm thinking,' answered Garrett.

'I say we wait until dark, sneak down there, kill everyone, get Freedom, go home,' suggested the Zulu.

Garrett grinned. 'It has its merits.'

'But?'

'But...there's thirty, forty, maybe fifty people down there.'

'So? We work fast. Kill quick.'

Garrett didn't answer. He stayed glued to the binoculars. Adjusted the focus slightly. 'The window is boarded up from the outside. Nailed into the frame. Do you think that you could lever it off with your assegai?'

Petrus nodded. 'Easy.'

'You sure?'

'Sure,' confirmed Petrus.

'Right. We wait here until dark and then we get closer. We hide up until later. Then we sneak down. I take up position in front of the barn doors. Shotgun and rifle. You get Freedom's window open. Quietly. If we can get away without a fight, all the better. But if things go wrong I'll open up on the barn. You get Freedom away. We meet back here at the pick-up.'

'Good plan,' agreed Petrus.

'But first,' continued Garrett. 'We find the guards.'

'What guards?'

'There'll be guards,' said Garrett. 'Trust me.' He continued scanning the surrounds. Searching. Probing. Seeking.

Finally. 'There. To the left of the water tower.' He passed the binoculars to Petrus.

'Well spotted. Some sort of bunker. Two people inside. Do you think that there are others?'

Garrett shook his head. 'I don't think that they expect anyone. I reckon it's some sort of training camp and sentries are set up as a matter of course. We keep an eye on them. After they change shifts we wait ten minutes and then kill them. Blades. Quick and quiet. Then we go in.'

The two of them lay still. And slowly, all around them the land shrouded itself in shadow. Gold turned to red then to purple and finally, blue-black.

The moon was close to full. An artist's palette rendered all in the various shades of death.

And through the muted landscape crawled two warriors. Come to claim their own.

***

Manhattan Dengana stood and let the applause wash over him. He had just been awarded the Order of the Baobab, Supreme Councilor class.

It hung around his neck on its cream and gold ribbon. A large, rough rectangle of gold with a graphic of the Baobab tree in the middle. For exceptional service in industry and economy.

Although the medal had been granted by the president himself, he had not actually attended the award ceremony. Dengana was too hot a political potato for that to ever happen. Ever since he had supported the new police commissioner, Bheki Cele in openly attempting to change the law to enable policemen to shoot to kill suspects without comeback or worry, he had been pushed to the side of the president's inner circle. This despite the fact that the president himself had announced a range of "tough" measures to deal with citizens protesting against poor services, and this year alone over one thousand people had died in police custody.

But Manhattan was not perturbed, because, in only a few more days, he would be one of the wealthiest men on the African continent. And the one thing that he had learnt was; the big dog always eats first.

He stepped down off the stage and started his rounds. Meeting and greeting. Shaking hands. Patting backs. Ministerial. Magnanimous.

'Congratulations, Dengana. Another medal. Soon you'll look like Idi Amin or Gaddafi.'

Manhattan turned to face his congratulator. 'Good evening colonel. I didn't know that you had been invited.'

Zuzani smiled. 'I wasn't. But it would take a brave doorman to refuse entrance to the colonel. Anyway, I naturally assumed that my lack of invitation was due to forgetfulness on your part. Very remiss of you, Dengana. Very remiss. Perhaps you should have your new personal assistant disciplined. Perhaps she should be reminded that I am an important part of your life. Some might even say, an integral part.' Zuzani shook his head. 'You see, I would hate us to become bad friends, Dengana. That would break my heart. And yours too.'

Manhattan leaned towards Zuzani, his voice low. 'Watch your tone of voice, colonel. Don't forget who you are. You work for me.'

Zuzani laughed. Genuine amusement. 'Oh, Manhattan, my good friend. I work *with* you, not *for* you. We are partners. Your good fortune is my good fortune. I am sure that you understand what I am saying.'

Manhattan took a deep breath. 'Are you threatening me?'

Zuzani shrugged. Said nothing.

'How dare you?' Continued Manhattan as he poked Zuzani in the chest with his finger. 'You gamble with your life. I know people. Bad people.'

Zuzani laughed again. 'No, Manhattan. You don't know bad people. You know me. I am your bad people. You are simply a fat, bloated, corrupt politician and if you ever jab me in the chest again I will come around to your house and cut your fingers off. But there is no need for all of this unpleasantness. We are friends. Partners. Trust me, I shall ensure that no harm comes to you. And, in return, you will ensure that my financial future remains both profitable and secure.' Zuzani patted Manhattan on the shoulder. 'Smile, Dengana. Life is good.' Then he turned away and left.

There was nothing that Manhattan could do. He had inadvertently allowed Zuzani to become too powerful. However, in contrast to chairman Mao, Dengana knew that power does not always grow from the barrel of a gun. Dengana knew that true power came through wealth, because with wealth, one could buy as many trigger fingers as one needed.

With a visible shake of his head Manhattan Dengana plastered a smile on his face, stood tall and carried on cruising the room, meeting and greeting.

***

The two warriors had crawled to within fifty feet of the sentry dugout. Here they waited. Silent as the surrounding night. Before they had started their advance, Garrett had torn two strips of material from his shirt. They had tied these around their mouths so that, when the temperature dropped, there would be no visible condensation in the air.

After three hours or so they saw two men walking towards the dugout. They appeared unarmed. As they approached the two current sentries stood up and greeted them. Then they handed over two sidearms. Pistols. There was some muted conversation and the two new sentries climbed into the dugout. The relieved pair walked back towards the dormitory barn.

Garrett glanced at his watch. It was one-forty-two in the morning. That meant one of two things. The fact that the sentries had been changed at an odd time as opposed to on the hour or half hour meant that they were very slack or, that their commander was very good. Only amateurs changed sentries on the hour. It was too easy to predict. Too easy to plan around.

He leaned close to Petrus. 'They don't have enough arms to go around. That's why they need the arms cache. Did you see, they transferred their weapons to the new sentries.'

Petrus nodded. The movement just recognizable in the moonlight. They waited another ten minutes. 'Right,' whispered Garrett. 'Let's do it.'

He drew his machete from its sheath and Petrus did the same with his assegai. The dull metal blades looked like black holes in the night. Apart from the sharpened edges which stood out as slivers of moonlight.

As slow as cancer the two warriors slid forward. Inch by measured inch.

And then it was as if the night came alive. A brief flurry of movement. Two wet thuds. Quiet. Still again.

The sharpened edges of the blades no longer reflected the moon. Blood covered the light. Deep red and viscous as honey.

They continued their approach. This time running softly. Bent double to present as little target as possible. Petrus went right and then dropped to the ground, crawling the last thirty feet to the boarded-up window.

Garrett went left and positioned himself on an angle between the front door of the farmhouse and the barn. That way he could cover both entrances. He lay prone, put the Protecta shotgun down in front of him, shouldered the assault rifle and waited.

Petrus crept along the wall until he was under the window. Then he paused. He was unsure whether to whisper for Freedom or simply lever off the boards. Both choices had their dangers. If someone else were in the room then they would hear him calling, and maybe shoot him through the board. But then, on the other hand, the same could happen if he simply pulled the boards off. He thought for a few seconds.

'Fuck it,' he whispered to himself as he pushed the blade of his assegai in between the board and the wall and started to pull. The wood squealed against the nails, cutting through the silence like a banshee. Petrus stopped. Waited. Started again…slowly, working at the tension with small tugs. Bouncing.

Garrett watched both doors.

It was no good. It would take Petrus all night, nibbling away at the fixings. So, he threw caution to the wind, pushed the blade in deeper and, with one mighty pull, tore the board off. The nails screeched again and the board clattered to the ground. Petrus looked into the window.

'Freedom?'

'Uncle,' replied Freedom. 'I knew that you would come.'

'Come on, nephew. Let's go. Move.'

The young Zulu clambered through the open window, falling to the ground. Petrus picked him up and they ran, bent over, in the direction of the pick-up.

Garrett was about to follow when the barn door burst open and two men appeared, both carried handguns. At the same time the door to the farmhouse sprang open and a man barreled out, a rifle in his hands. Garrett took a quick snap shot at the man outside the farmhouse. Missed. The man dropped and rolled. Garrett swiveled back to the barn. Two quick shots. Center of body mass. Both down. Back to the man from the farmhouse. Gone. More men came pouring out of the barn. Six. Seven. Eight. Garrett lay down the assault rifle, picked up the Protecta and fired. Fast. Twelve rounds in four seconds. The men were all unarmed. They died. Garrett killed them. The beast threw back its head and howled. Reveling in its freedom. Colors grew more intense. The night welcomed him home. And all compassion and quarter ceased to exist.

He snatched up the assault rifle and fired into the barn quick double taps until the thirty round mag was empty. He dropped the mag. Replaced with a new one. Stood up and ran.

He heard rifle fire behind him. The bullet passed close enough to ruffle his hair. The next one clipped his bicep. Fire ran through his body. He jinked left, then right. Sprinting hard. Another round kicked up dust at his feet.

'Fuck,' he grunted. 'This dude is good.'

He hit the ground. Rolled. Spun around. Fired five rounds. Got up and ran again. Her could see Petrus and Freedom in front of him. Freedom was struggling and

Petrus was half carrying him as they ran. He could hear running feet behind him.

Something struck him in the thigh. A hammer blow. His leg flicked out from under him and he went down hard. He saw Petrus stop. Turn. He was coming back for him.

'No,' shouted Garrett. 'Go. Just fucking go.'

All around him the night air was torn apart with the whip and slap of passing shot. Petrus came closer, arms pumping, silhouetted perfectly against the moon.

Blood sprayed high. Black against the moonlight sky. Petrus' head snapped back. He stood still for almost a second and then fell to the floor. His legs twitched slightly and then he was still.

Garrett screamed wordlessly. An animal cry. Atavistic and primal. He rose up on one knee and shouldered the rifle. The first three shots took out the closest three pursuers.

'Run,' he shouted over his shoulder. 'Run, Freedom. The keys are in the pick-up. Run.'

He worked from left to right and back again. Saw men going down. Ran dry. Reloaded. Fire. Fire. Traverse. Fire again. All around him bullets struck. So close that he could feel them. He was hit in his side, the round traveling through. In and out. Another round clipped his torso. Ricocheted off, smashing a rib as it did.

But the beast laughed and scorned such trivial wounds.

He reloaded again. Last magazine. Aim and fire. Aim and fire.

A bullet struck a rock in front of him, spun off and struck him in the chest. It didn't penetrate the bone but it knocked the wind out of him.

His rifle clicked empty.

He was still screaming.

Men. All around.

He tried to stand.

A rifle butt hit him in the face.

And another.

Another.

Stars.

Lights.

Black.

CHAPTER NINETEEN

They buried Sifiso's mama the next morning. Early. Just after sunrise. The surrounding gravestones were covered in dew. Tiny silver spheres that refracted the rising sun into myriads of miniature rainbows.

There was no priest but the staff had provided a simple wooden cross that marked the grave. If she had been buried in the pauper's section, she would not have been allowed a marker.

Sifiso asked Kobus to say something. But the big man was not religious. So, he said the only words that he knew. The ones that the army chaplain always recited to them before battle.

'Bow down your heavens, o Lord, and come down; touch the mountains, and they shall smoke. Flash forth lightning and scatter them; shoot your arrows and destroy them. Stretch out your hand and rescue me and deliver me from the hand of foreigners whose mouths speak lying words and whose right hand is falsehood. Amen.'

Sifiso had joined in with the amen. And smiled. Words had been said. This was good.

On the way back to the squatter camp Kobus had purchased a live goat with some of the money that had been left over from bribing the funeral officials.

The goat was as undernourished as the two of them. Skin, bone, ragged fur.

They slaughtered and dressed it in front of Kobus' hut. Cooked it over open flames. Traditionally they were meant to burn all of mama's possessions to go with her to the afterlife. But she had none. Not even a change of clothes. Instead, they burnt the grass mat that had lain on the floor of their shack. Sifiso also cut off some of his hair and threw that into the fire to symbolize the fact that part of him had also died.

Then they had shared the goat meat with the surrounding squatters. Tiny, rank pieces of underdone flesh.

And so, it was done. Propriety had been adhered to. Tradition had been observed.

Mama was gone.

***

Pitch black. Garrett squeezed his eyes shut until little blooms of color rippled across his vision. Then he opened them wide. Nothing.

He wondered if he had gone blind. Where was he? Memories staggered back into his consciousness. Shooting. Running. Blood, arcing through the night sky.

Petrus was dead.

He tried to move but couldn't. He had been re-strained completely. Sitting down. Probably tied to a chair. Or duct taped. Immobile.

Petrus was dead.

Pain throbbed through his body. Every heartbeat tolled out a wave of hurt. He felt his teeth with his tongue. Loose. Left hand incisor broken off. A ragged stump.

Petrus was dead.

Something small and urgent ran over him. Rat. Then another. Spiky claws dug into his chest. The feral smell filled his nostrils. It bit into his chest. He couldn't move.

Petrus was dead.

He screamed at the rat. Voice hoarse from lack of water. The rodent chattered back at him and scurried off. Little pinpricks traveling down his body. Started gnawing on his boot.

An explosion of light. A door opening. The rats scuttled away. Someone walked into the room. Steps slow and steady.

The door shut behind him. Relief. He wasn't blind.

A match lit up the darkness. A tiny supernova in a universe of black. A cigarette being dragged on

Each drag lit up the person's face with a dull orange glow. A big man. Rough shaven. Scar that crawled down the side of his face. Eyes, deep set. Orbs of ob-sidian.

He said nothing. Merely stared. Garrett wasn't sure how much the man could see by the light of his own cigarette. The man stepped forward; cigarette clenched in his teeth. Swung his fist.

Garrett's world exploded in pain.

Darkness.

When he came to again it was still pitch black. The rat still gnawing on his boot. Tough English leather. Something was crawling around on his back, underneath his shirt. Spider? Beetle?

His tongue was swollen from lack of moisture. He wondered how long he had been there. A day? Week? Perhaps. Probably not.

'Hello?' His voice rasped, producing a croak. Not an intelligible word. He tried again. 'Water. Anyone.'

The pain had become more localized. He could feel individual areas. His thigh. His side. His breastbone. His bicep. His face...all of it.

The door creaked open. This time a little light came in. Nighttime outside. Or maybe early morning. The same big man walked in. He had a tin mug of water. Walked over to Garrett, held it to his lips and tilted. Garrett sucked on it, bolting it down in fear that it might be pulled away. But it wasn't.

Its effect was instant. Relative strength flowed through him. The minimal light from the door also brought with it hope.

The big man lit himself a cigarette. 'You killed some of my boys,' he said. His voice was deep. His accent guttural. And he emanated a palpable feeling of power. A life force that seemed to surround him like a nimbus. Garrett knew instantly who he was.

'The Prophet.'

The man raised an eyebrow. 'You know me?'

'I know of you,' Garrett croaked. 'I know what people say.'

'And what do people say?'

'That you are insane.'

The man shrugged. 'They may be right. I do sometimes wonder myself.' He took out another cigarette, lit it and placed it between Garrett's broken lips. Garrett inhaled hard. Thankful for the nicotine.

'And who are you, soldier boy?' The man asked.

Garrett said nothing. Inhaled. Let the smoke trickle out through his nostrils.

'Are you a friend of the kaffir that we shot? Or are you professional help?'

Still Garrett remained silent. Dust motes danced in the cigarette smoke; spot lit by the light coming in from the door. Fairy lights.

'Freedom got away,' said the man.

Garrett allowed himself a tiny smile. A mere twitch of the lips.

'So, now I need to know, are you a family friend or not?'

Garrett knew why. They needed a new hostage. If he was simply professional help then he was of no use to them. If, however, he was a friend of the family then he might be worth something as a bargaining chip. Whatever, the best thing to do was to keep quiet. Even though he knew that it would cost him.

The man leaned closer. 'So, not feeling talkative? Don't worry, soon you will.' He backhanded Garrett across the face. A solid blow that knocked him and his chair over sideways. He lay on the floor. Immobile.

The man left the room, not bothering to close the door behind him.

Garrett could see that it was darkening outside. So, he knew it was early evening. He tried moving but was taped too tightly to the chair. He could still hear the rats scuttling around in the corners of the room. But for the moment they had been scared away. When night fell, he knew they would be back.

After an hour or so he drifted off to sleep, his exhaustion winning over his fear of the rats.

***

Garrett awoke with a start. It was dark. Not pitch black but still very dark

Something had woken him up. A sound. He strained his ears. Then he heard it and his heart dropped. An abrupt yelp followed by a succession of shorter yelps. Close. Very close. Mere yards from the open door.

A sound that he had last heard when he had been fighting in Somalia in the late nineties. It was the sound of a black-backed jackal. A small foxlike animal.

Brazen scavengers and hunters, they were known to be carriers of diseases like rabies and distemper.

He shivered with dread. He had seen people die of rabies before. Far from medical help. Before they died the virus drove them insane. Delusions and paranoia, hallucinations, mind numbing terror and acute hydrophobia. Even the mention of water would send them into paroxysms of fear and fury. And even if the animal was not diseased it was no mere rat. It could chew his face off without any problem at all. While all that he could do was lie on the floor, strapped to a chair.

The jackal yelped again and then he could hear it snuffling. Getting closer and closer to the open door. There was a flicker in the moonlight and it was in the room with him. He could see it silhouetted against the open door. It skulked towards him; head held low.

Garrett threw everything he had into breaking free. He flicked his head back and forth, strained at his bonds and tried, desperately, to kick his legs free.

The jackal, seeing him struggle, started to growl. Low and deep. He inched forward; lips peeled back.

And the right leg broke off the chair. Garrett kicked back and forth until he had torn his leg free then he pulled it up to his chest and booted the jackal as hard as he could in the snout. The animal struck the wall and bounced back, straight into a savage cross kick that landed just behind its head. The sound of its neck breaking was audible above the thump of the kick. The dead body slid down the wall to the floor. Garrett struggled to get his breath. Lights pin wheeled across his vision and his heart hammered in his chest like a trapped animal.

He glanced across at the dead jackal. Already five or six rats were feeding on it. Heads bobbing up and down as they tore at the still warm flesh. Chattering with excitement.

The effort proved too much for Garrett in his weakened state and he passed out again.

CHAPTER TWENTY

That morning someone came into the room and fed Garrett two cups of water. However, because he was still lying on the floor, most of it simply spilled down his face. The person didn't speak. Nor did he move the body of the jackal and, as the day wore on, the carcass started to rot. The stench filled the small airless room like a miasma.

Much later, after the sun had gone down for another night, The Prophet appeared at the door with a younger man. They entered the room and stared at Garrett. Pete spoke first.

'It appears that your friends don't give a shit about you. I texted them and told them it was your life or the arms cache. I have given them two days and they haven't bothered to answer.'

Garrett craned his neck to look at The Prophet. He said nothing. There was no point.

'So,' Pete continued. 'This here is Cornelius. Three days ago, you killed his younger brother whilst rescuing the kaffir. His brother's name was Bismarck. He was nineteen. I am going to leave you with Cornelius so that you can learn the error of your ways.'

'Fuck you,' said Garrett. His voice almost a whisper. 'Fuck you very much, you psychopathic nutcase.'

The Prophet went down on one knee before Garrett. With his two hands he took his face and turned it towards him. His eyes burned into Garrett's like a spiritual fire. An almost unearthly charisma. 'And for your lifeblood I will require a reckoning: from every beast I will require it, and from man. From his fellow man I will require a reckoning for the life of man. Whoever sheds the blood of man, by man shall his blood be shed, for God made man in his own image. Genesis, chapter nine, versus five and six.'

He stood up and walked out.

Cornelius stepped over and kicked Garrett in the face. Not too hard. Hard enough to hurt like hell, but not hard enough to knock him out. Then he lit a cigarette. Smoked it down to the filter. Leant over and stubbed it out in Garrett's ear. The red-hot tip sizzled and spat as it burned into the tender flesh. Garrett clenched his jaw to prevent himself crying out in pain.

Then the young Afrikaner pulled out a knife from his belt. It was a simple blade. A workingman's knife. Perhaps six inches long. An inch wide sloping to a point. A leather-bound handle. He stood over Garrett.

'This was my brother's knife. He always carried it with him. It was like part of him. An extension almost. I am going to remove your eyes with this knife. His knife. And then I am going to place them, on your chest. Then I shall leave you here. In this room, with the rats. First, they will eat your eyes. Pulling them from your chest like a pair of meatballs. Then they will start on your eye sockets. Tearing at them with their little teeth. Pushing their heads inside. Feasting on your face. Your eyelids. Your brain. You will die in absolute agony. Absolute. And it will have been my brother's knife that did it. Remember that when you are dying. Remember my brother.'

He took a step forward. There was a thud. Like the sound of someone hitting a heavy punch bag. Cornelius frowned. Looked down at his chest. Two feet of dull red, razor-sharp assegai stuck out of it. There was a sucking sound as it withdrew and the young Afrikaner fell to the floor.

And behind him, picked out by the meager light coming in through the open door, stood a man with a bloody bandage around his head. He raised the assegai again and brought it down, swiftly slashing the tape that held Garrett captive. Then he bent down and helped him to his feet.

'Petrus?'

'The very man himself,' answered the Zulu.

'I knew that you were alive.'

Petrus chuckled. 'No, you didn't. Come on. Quick, let's blow this joint.'

Garrett staggered along next to Petrus who held his elbow in one hand, steadying him. The moon was bright enough to see by, blue highlights and black shadows. The door to the farmhouse opened and a man stepped out. Not The Prophet. Someone younger. He stood just outside the open door; the interior light spilled over him covering him in a gentle yellow glow.

Garrett and Petrus froze. There wasn't time to go to ground so they simply stood still. A shadow amongst many other shadows. The man delved into his trouser pocket and pulled out a pack of cigarettes. He shook one loose, replaced the pack and pulled out a Zippo. Flicked. Lit. At the same time he saw them. He dropped the Zippo and pulled a pistol from his belt.

'Move!' Shouted Petrus. They both started to run. But they were slow, even though Petrus was dragging Garrett by the arm their progress limited to the speed of Garrett's loose-limbed stagger. The man started firing at them. Bullets buzzed past. Spiteful lead insects.

Then there was the sharp crack of an assault rifle. The man spun around and dropped to the ground. Kobus stood up, appearing out of the dark, beckoning to them.

'Come on, guys. Let's keep moving.'

He grabbed Garrett's other arm and they kept running. A cripple with a homemade wooden foot, a man with three bullet wounds and a Zulu prince with an assegai. It was only a matter of time before they were caught.

More men ran out of the farmhouse. They were all armed and started firing at once. Dust kicked up around the running trio and the air around them was savagely torn apart from passing shot. A bullet clipped Garrett high up on his right shoulder, taking out a chunk of flesh and spraying the three of them with blood.

'Ah, shit,' said Garrett. 'I've been shot again. I'm really getting sick of this.'

Then, with a shout of surprise, Kobus fell over, hitting the ground hard.

'What?' Asked Petrus. 'Have you been hit?'

Kobus shook his head, he held up his wooden appendage. 'Straps broke. Shit.'

'Can you still walk?' asked Petrus.

Kobus grinned. 'Don't be stupid. You mean hop away?'

Petrus held out his hand. Come on, grab my hand and lean against me. We can make it.'

Kobus shook his head. 'No ways, man. We do that then we're all screwed. Go. Quick, they're getting closer. I'll cover you guys.'

Petrus shook his head. 'No.'

A bullet whined off a rock next to Kobus. Missed him by a matter of inches.

'Just fuck off, Petrus. Please.'

Petrus squeezed Kobus' hand. 'Stay in peace, my friend.'

'One thing, take care of little Sifiso.'

'I will.'

'Promise.'

'I swear.'

'Good, now go.'

Petrus and Garrett turned and continued to move. Kobus lay down, checked his magazine was seated properly and started to lay down carefully gauged suppressive fire, causing their pursuers to go to ground.

In 1939 when the Berbers fought the modern Italian army in Libya, the tribesmen, facing overwhelming odds, used to tie their legs together before the battle thus forcing them to keep firing their rifles until the enemy was on top of them. No chance to retreat.

Basically, Kobus had done the same thing as he lay next to his broken wooden leg. He counted each round as he fired. Looking more to slow the advance down than to take life. Firing off to the sides to stop them flanking him. Waiting as long as he could between each shot.

Finally, he counted that he had one shot left. Using the rifle as a crutch he dragged himself onto his one knee and placed the barrel under his chin.

'Forgive me my sins, O Lord; forgive me the sins of my youth and the sins of mine age, the sins of my soul and the sins of my body, my secret and my whispering sins, the sins I have done to please myself and the sins I have done to please others. Forgive those sins that I know, and the sins that I know not; forgive them, O Lord, please forgive them all.'

He pulled the trigger.

Kobus' sacrifice had allowed Garrett and Petrus time to get to the pick-up. Petrus bundled his wounded friend into the passenger seat, jumped behind the wheel and took off fast, the truck skidding from side to side as it gained traction.

Neither of them said anything for a while. Silence while Petrus concentrated on driving hard and fast. Eventually they hit the blacktop road and things got easier.

'Right,' said Garrett. 'What the hell happened?'

'Thanks, Petrus. Good to see you,' said the Zulu.

Garrett grinned, leaned over and grasped Petrus by the shoulder. 'I'm sorry. Thanks, my friend. I owe you.'

'No problem. Petrus pulled a pack of cigarettes out. Drove one handed. Passed the pack to Garrett. 'Light us up.'

Garrett obliged. Lit two. Put one in Petrus' mouth. Petrus cracked the window.

'Right,' he said. 'After I got shot and you went down, Freedom dragged me to the pick-up. Basically, carried me. He's strong that one, I tell you. He thought that I was dying but it turns out that they just shot my ear off. Was hanging on by a few shreds of skin. Creased my skull. Knocked me out but good. Lots of blood.'

'Must look like shit,' said Garrett.

'No way. They sewed it back on. It's a bit crooked but I think that it gives me some character. You know. A slight flaw to attract attention to my otherwise flaw-less looks.'

They were both talking lightly. Teasing. Neither wanted to talk about the obvious. Eventually Garrett brought it up.

'Kobus died for us.'

'For sure. When I asked for his help, he didn't even hesitate. He's a good man. *Was* a good man.'

Neither of them spoke for a while. An unsaid moment of silence for a man they barely knew. A wasted cripple of a man who lived alone and took care of a small child who was not his. A good man.

Petrus flicked his cigarette stub out of the window. 'I sent Freedom and his family to my father's village in The Valley of a Thousand Hills. My father's warriors will protect them all. Any of these fuckers try to take on the children of the sky they'll all end up dead with an assegai up their ass.'

'Good move,' said Garrett. His voice was slurred and his head lolled back and forth from exhaustion.

'Rest, my friend. We'll be on the road for many hours now. Sleep.'

Garrett slept.

CHAPTER TWENTY-ONE

The man that delivered the maps of the Parliamentary Union buildings to Pete Vermulen stood in front of Manhattan Dengana. He was a nobody. A mere deliverer of messages. A go between that Manhattan used to liaise with The Prophet. His only advantage was that he was white. Pete would never have dealt with a black man. He would have known that something was wrong. He would have known that he was being played. That he was a mere piece in a game far beyond his understanding. The game of thrones where money trumped all. Manhattan had used his white lackey to convince Pete that he had sympathetic backers for his cause. Right wing backers. White supremacists. It had not been easy; Manhattan had had to play Pete like a giant game fish. With both strength and patience. Because the Prophet was, by his very nature, a suspicious person. But Pete had wanted to believe. He had wanted to believe more than anything. And his natural paranoia had been washed aside by the waves of his need for a white homeland.

But now none of that mattered. Unless Manhattan could do some serious damage control then there would be no arms cache. There would be no attempted coup.

There would be no one billion-dollar payout.

'When did mister Vermulen contact you?' Asked Manhattan.

'Half an hour ago. I came straight here. He told me that they no longer had Freedom in custody and that he had been attacked on two separate occasions. He has suffered almost fifty percent casualties. Eighteen of his men dead or injured.

Manhattan thought for a while. 'We shall have to take the rest of the family. Freedom's mother and father. I was trying to avoid that. It will complicate things because who will organize the collection of the arms caches?'

Isaac said nothing.

'You are dismissed,' continued Manhattan. 'I'll call if I need you.'

He was on the phone before Isaac had even left the room.

'Colonel, how are you? I need a small job done. The customary rates will apply. Please could you send some of your men around to Sipho Mabena's house and arrest him and any family members who happen to be there. Take them to the usual place, I'll see you there.'

***

Garrett grunted as the doctor pulled the final stitch tight. He had wrapped Garrett's chest to support the broken rib, cleaned and stitched the wound in his thigh and packed the shoulder wound with a mixture of Betadine and sugar and stuck a pressure bandage on. Rudimentary care to say the very least but Garrett felt a thousand times better.

Petrus had driven them to a lean-to house in the middle of the Alexandra Township. A mere two rooms, outside latrine. No running water. A single iron bed. A wooden chair.

The doctor gave Garrett a handful of painkillers and he washed them down with water.

'So,' said Garrett. 'It's done. What now?'

'Now, you wait here, you need to heal up a bit. There's no chance of you flying with all of those holes in you. Rest. I'm going to find this Sifiso kid and get him to my father's village. They'll take care of him there.'

Garrett lay back on the bed, closed his eyes and almost immediately fell asleep.

Petrus left the room.

The doctor sat down in the wooden chair, took a battered Agatha Christie novel out of his case and started to read.

CHAPTER TWENTY-TWO

Colonel Zuzani lounged in the wingback chair, his legs thrust out in front of him, his body slouched down. A picture of insouciance. In his hand an unlit cigar.

'What do you mean, there is no one there?' asked Manhattan.

The colonel studied his unlit cigar for a while. 'Why don't they pre-cut these things? I mean, really, would it take them that much longer? The fucking things cost me over one hundred American dollars each and I've got to cut the end off myself.' He took a small silver cigar cutter out of his jacket pocket and snipped the cap off his Behika, letting the off-cut fall to the floor. He replaced the cutter, took out a gold Dunhill and warmed the foot of the cigar, turning as he did so. Finally, he put it in his mouth and drew it to flame. Then he studied the burning tip, a look of satisfaction on his face. A job well done.

'Where are they?' Continued Manhattan.

'Gone,' said the colonel. 'I already told you.'

Manhattan controlled himself with visible strain. 'Gone where, colonel?'

Zuzani rolled the cigar smoke around in his mouth. Exhaled. 'I can't be sure, but if I had to guess, and I believe that you would like me to, I would guess that they have gone to Chief Dlamini's village.'

'So? Go and get them.'

Zuzani laughed. 'What? Are you insane? It would be suicide.'

'Why? You have fifty men, an armored car. A fucking helicopter.'

'Yes, and chief Dlamini has access to over ten thousand shields. I wouldn't pit my men against one thousand *amadota* let alone ten thousand. Face it, Dengana, you're going to have to find another way to make your plan work.'

Manhattan thought for a while. Let his mind roam. The cigar smoke twisted and turned its way around the room. A mystical snake of gray and blue and white.

'We have to find Petrus Dlamini,' he said. 'If we can capture him, then we can use him as leverage to get the arms cache.'

The colonel nodded. 'True.'

'So,' continued Manhattan. 'Go and get him.'

Zuzani stared at Dengana for a while. His eyes hooded. Unreadable.

'Please,' he said.

'What?'

'Say please.'

Manhattan took a deep breath. 'Please.'

Zuzani stood up. 'There, see. Good manners cost nothing.'

He strode from the room, trailing smoke like a warship.

Manhattan gritted his teeth. The colonel was starting to become a liability. His arrogance was beginning to outweigh his usefulness. However, he was Manhattan's strong arm. So, as such, Manhattan had no one that he could use to take out Zuzani. And the colonel knew this so, it was only a matter of time before he used his military strength to usurp Manhattan's place in the hierarchy.

Manhattan picked up the phone and dialed Doberman security.

'Sampson Sabelo. It's Manhattan here. Manhattan Dengana. How would you like to get back at Petrus Dlamini and his friend?'

*****

Garrett woke to find a small child standing next to the bed staring at him. His eyes were wide. He was drinking from a can of Fanta with a straw.

'Hello, man,' he said.

'Hello, boy.'

'You were asleep.'

'Yes,' agreed Garrett. 'I was.' He climbed off the bed, stood up. Ran his fingers through his dark hair, pulling out the knots, letting it tumble in loose waves to his shoulders. He stretched. Winced as his injuries pulled up tight. The dull light threw his musculature into stark relief. Twisted cords of muscle. Abs like packed concrete. Scars that crisscrossed his torso like a child's scribbling. A body courtesy of Mars, the god of war. As opposed to Abercrombie and Fitch, the gods of metrosexuality.

'The doctor is gone. Petrus is coming back soon,' continued the child. 'My name is Sifiso. My mama is dead. So is my friend, the big man.' He held out his can of Fanta. 'Do you want some?'

Garrett shook his head. 'No thanks, Sifiso.' He pulled on his shirt and then extracted a pack from the pocket. Picked one. Lit. Sat down on the edge of the bed.

Sifiso kept staring at him. It was disconcerting.

'What happened to you?' asked the boy.

'I got shot.'

'Are you going to die?'

Garrett smiled. 'No.'

'Maybe?'

'Definitely not.'

'Good.'

Garrett glanced at his watch.

'I can tell the time,' said Sifiso.

'Really?'

'No. I don't have a watch. But if I did have a watch, I think that I would be able to tell the time.'

He went over to the chair. Sat down, swinging his legs.

'I'm sorry about your mama,' said Garrett. 'And the big man.'

Sifiso shrugged. 'It wasn't your fault.'

Garrett lent over and laid his hand on Sifiso's shoulder. An attempt to convey his feelings. His debt to the big man. His sorrow that this orphaned child's only protector had died saving him. Sifiso's bones felt like a bundle of twigs. Fragile. Vulnerable.

The little boy smiled at him and then concentrated on sucking the last drops of Fanta pop out of the can.

The door opened and Petrus walked in. He was carrying a large tote bag that he dumped on the floor. There was a metallic clink as he did so.

'Feeling better?'

Garrett shrugged. 'Better than what?'

Petrus laughed. 'I've made a plan for Sifiso. He's going to my father's village. They'll take care of him. We need to give him a lift to Ladysmith. It's a few hours from here. Someone will pick him up there. We'll meet them outside a convenience store called Christina's. It's on the main drag.'

The three of them trooped out of the dwelling. They didn't lock the door. Petrus carried the bag with him, bundled it onto the back seat of the cab next to Sifiso.

They pulled off, stopping just outside the city to fill up with gas and to buy some cigarettes and food. Sifiso slept for most of the way, waking up every now and then to point at something next to the road and voice his opinion.

'Look. Mountains. I've never been on a mountain,' or 'Cows. Many cows. Also, sheep. See?' Garrett or Petrus would grunt in return and then Sifiso, happy to get a response would go back to sleep for a while.

When they arrived at the rendezvous point, they were met by two Zulu men and a woman. Petrus had a brief chat and then Sifiso was transferred to their car. An old, mustard yellow Ford Cortina. As they drove off Sifiso waved at them through the back window until they were out of sight.

CHAPTER TWENTY-THREE

Despite his casual attitude towards Manhattan Dengana, colonel Zuzani had been hard at work since he had left Dengana's office. He had leaned firmly on a few of his local informers and had learnt that Petrus had last been seen leaving Alexandra in a white pick-up with another two people inside. A white man and a small child.

He phoned major Goso who was in charge of highway patrols and asked him to put out an APB but not to arrest anyone. Simply tell Zuzani of their whereabouts.

He didn't have to wait long. The pick-up had been spotted on its way back to Johannesburg without the child on board.

Zuzani picked up his desk phone and pushed the intercom button. Sergeant Fumba answered.

'Sergeant. Organize a roadblock on the N3 highway. Put it on the stretch of road just past the Suikerbosrant River. We'll stop them before they get to Heidelberg. Take the Casspir and twenty men. Try to take Petrus alive. Do what you want to the whitey. Move.'

Fumba ran downstairs, talking on his cell as he did. Issuing orders. It would take around forty minutes to get to the area and twenty to round up the men. It would be close but they would make it.

***

The sun was setting. Heat rose off the blacktop in shimmers, bending the light cast by the lowering sun. Mirages of red and scarlet djinns danced across the road. Patches of faux water appeared and disappeared in front of them as they drove. Illusions of moisture in a landscape of dust.

Petrus wound his window down and blasted himself with fresh air.

'Well,' he said. 'It's over. Freedom is safe. The family is safe. We're alive. Maybe you book into a hotel for a few days, let the stitches take. Then, time for you to go home.'

Garrett grunted his agreement.

'Don't sound so happy,' teased Petrus.

'I'm happy,' replied Garrett. 'I was just thinking, every time that I see you, I get shot. Maybe next time you come to Scotland. It's safer there.'

'Nowhere is safe with you,' said Petrus.

And then, out of the mirages, loomed a huge armored vehicle parked across the highway. It was painted in the yellow and blue livery of the South

Africa police force. Standing next to it were at least twenty well-armed men in full combat gear.

There was very little other traffic on the road and the few cars that were in front of the pick-up were waved around the armored vehicle without inspection. However, as Petrus approached the armed men all trained their rifles on the pick-up and a man, sporting captain's pips, held up his hand, commanding them to halt.

'Oh, shit,' said Petrus. 'This is trouble.'

Without hesitation he rammed his foot flat on the gas and yanked the steering wheel hard right. The pick-up leapt forward and ramped off the side of the high-way into the surrounding veld. Petrus kept his foot down and the pick-up jumped and bucked across the open scrubland.

Behind them the men opened up but the bullets flew wide. Almost as if they weren't trying to hit them. Petrus glanced in his rear-view mirror. The Casspir armored vehicle had pulled off the road and was in hot pursuit. This didn't bother Petrus much, as long as the terrain didn't get too rough then he had the edge on speed. As long as they didn't break down or come across any impassable obstacle.

'Why are we running?' asked Garrett. 'Maybe it was just a routine roadblock.'

'No way,' answered Petrus. 'Firstly, there are almost no routine roadblocks any more. The cops would rather sit around doing fuck-all. And, secondly, they were looking for us. They didn't even glance at the other cars but as soon as we showed up the captain got all excited. I'm telling you, we're in shit with the cops somehow. This is not good.'

'But how?'

'Well, we have shot up a few people.'

'Granted, but they were as illegal as us. It doesn't make sense.'

'Can't think now. Gotta drive.'

Petrus concentrated and kept going. After twenty minutes they came across a dirt road leading to no-where. He pulled onto it and within another ten minutes they had lost the Casspir completely.

Petrus slowed down to less breakneck speed.

Garrett lit a couple of cigarettes. Passed one over. 'They weren't trying to kill us,' he said.

'You think?'

'For sure. They had a 7.62 machinegun mounted on their vehicle. If they'd opened up with that…well, goodnight sweet prince.'

'True. So how does that help us?'

'Well, why would they want us alive?'

Petrus thought for a while. 'Shit. The Prophet. He's behind this. Must be. He wants the weapons cache and figures that we're the only way to it. There's no way that he would take on my father and his *impi* so he's gunning for us.'

Garrett shook his head. 'No. As I said before, doesn't make sense. I mean, let's look at this logically.

A group of black policemen hunting us down on behalf of a group of white supremacists in order to capture us so that the supremacists can get hold of a shitload of weapons. No way.'

They drove in silence for a while.

'Where are we going?' Asked Garrett.

'Back to Alexandra,' answered Petrus.

'Not sure if we'll be safe there,' said Garrett. 'Any chance of hanging out at your father's place for a while until we sort this out?'

Petrus shook his head. 'As you may remember from the last time, I'm not my father's favorite person. He'll simply escort us to his borders and then we're fucked. No, we go back to Alexandra. Hide out in the middle. Cops aren't welcomed there. We'll be safe. Maybe.'

Maybe?'

'Maybe,' confirmed Petrus.

'Great,' sighed Garrett.

CHAPTER TWENTY-FOUR

Manhattan put the phone down. He couldn't believe it. Somehow that idiot, sergeant Fumba, had managed to lose Petrus Dlamini and the white man. A squad car had seen the pick-up heading towards the Alexandra Township and Zuzani was rallying his forces for a second attempt at capturing the two fugitives.

Dengana massaged his temples with both hands and sighed long and loud. Then he looked up at the man who was standing opposite his desk. Isaac Peterson stood at ease. A military posture. His gaze on some point above Manhattan's head.

'Isaac, I want you to contact Pete Vermulen. Tell him to bring four of his best men here.' Dengana flicked a note page across his desk. On it an address of a building supply company in Krugersdorp. Yet another of the many businesses that he owned. 'Take these as well,' he threw a set of car keys. Isaac caught them. 'Downstairs, right of the front door there's a blue panel van. In the back are five CR-21 assault rifles, three thousand rounds of ammunition and fifteen extra magazines. I want you to give them to mister

Vermulen. Tell him that they are on loan from his benefactor. Then tell him that Petrus Dlamini is hiding out in Alexandra. He needs to take him alive so that we can get the arms cache. Don't tell him about colonel Zuzani. We can still do this. Go.'

Isaac jogged off without question. The perfect messenger.

***

Petrus pulled over to the side of the road on the outskirts of Alexandra and killed the lights.

'Come on,' he said. 'We walk from here.' He grabbed the tote bag from the back seat, leaving the keys in the ignition. The two of them set off, the Zulu in the lead. 'They'll be looking for the pick-up,' he continued. 'With the keys there it'll be gone inside the hour.'

They walked down Arkwright Avenue. Above them yellow sodium streetlights hissed and buzzed. Perhaps one in every three working. The air was thick with smoke, acrid and heavy. Rising from over ten thousand cooking fires. Not only coal or wood but anything that burnt. Tires, old rags, plastic containers. The sodium lights washed the smog with bile. The color of disease.

Petrus took a right turn. Walking in between shacks. Weaving his way toward the top end of the township. There were no overhead lights here. Only the fires and the smoke. Shadows of people flickered around the fires. A strange mixture of two-bedroom houses, falling to ruin and corrugated iron and cardboard shacks leaning up against them. Covering almost every available piece of ground save for a small cooking area outside each one.

A long row of chemical toilets loomed out of the smog. All of them had overflowed and raw human waste had formed a gross, seething pool around them. The stench from them was eye-watering, bludgeoning the smell of the smoke and assailing the nostrils of anyone close.

Petrus continued. Eventually they came to a large red brick building. A long four-story block, its ends invisible in the smoke. It looked like a prison block.

'We'll be safe here,' said the Zulu.

'What is this place?'

'It's a hostel. Back in the days of apartheid the government built single-sex hostels for the migrant laborers. This one is controlled by the Zulus. Okay, take my lead, don't talk unless I tell you to. These places are bad news.'

'So why are we going in?'

'Because they hate the cops. Right, before we go in.'

Petrus lay the tote bag on the ground and unzipped it. He passed Garrett his machete and shoulder holster. Garrett took off his jacket, slipped the holster on and replaced his jacket. Petrus did the same with his assegai. Then he pulled out a CR-21 assault rifle and the Protecta shotgun. He handed the rifle, two extra magazines and five boxes of ammunition to Garrett.

Garrett loaded the two extra magazines and tucked them into his belt. Then he distributed the rest of the ammo around his pockets, trying to even out the weight. Finally, he checked his magazine was seated properly, racked a round into the chamber and drew a deep breath. Compartmentalizing his pain. Wrapping in a ball and burying it deep inside. Not merely ignoring it, actually causing its cessation. It was a great skill, but it took energy. And it could only be maintained for short periods of time.

They stood up and walked towards the entrance, leaving the empty bag where it was. They walked into the front lobby of the building. Inside were a group of five young men. They wore cheap Chinese knock-off Adidas, fake Rolex watches, ropes of gold-plated jewelry. They were all visibly armed. Shoulder holsters worn ostentatiously on the outside of their jackets. Each firearm was different; the only similarity was the bling. Some were chromed, others gold plated. Beaver tails, carbon fiber grips, laser sites and compensators abounded. Pimp my pistol. They all wore Ray-Ban Aviators.

They were involved in an animated conversation that drew to a swift close when Petrus and Garrett walked in, openly carrying an assault rifle and a semi-automatic shotgun.

Petrus took control. 'Hey,' he pointed at one of the men. 'You, we are here to see Fat Man. Go and tell him.'

'Why? Who are you to tell me what to do?' said the young man, deciding to show a bit of bravado in front of his friends.

Petrus smiled. A shark exposing its teeth to a clown fish. 'I am Petrus Dlamini, son of chief Dlamini. Why, who are you?'

The man held up his hands and shook his head. 'It doesn't matter who I am, I am sorry. I'll go and find Fat Man now. Please wait.'

He scuttled off.

'Nice to find such well-mannered young men, isn't it?' asked Petrus of Garrett.

'Very nice,' agreed Garrett. 'It warms the heart.'

'Petrus nodded. 'Perhaps I won't kill him when he gets back. Perhaps.' He winked at Garrett.

'See how you feel,' said Garrett. 'No need to rush the decision.'

The rest of the young men had huddled together in the corner of the lobby. The room was banter free; the lively conversation replaced with a fear-filled silence. Respect.

After a short while the messenger came running into the room. 'Please come with me, Fat Man will see you now.'

They followed him along the badly lit corridor. The air was full of smoke and smelled strongly of marijuana and stale beer. They could hear mumbled conversations behind the doors that they passed. At the end of the corridor was another door. Two men stood in front of it. These were not the Hollywood-style bad boys from the lobby; these two men were the real deal. Lean faced, grizzled and wearing simple dark clothes. One carried a sawn-off pump action shotgun and the other an old AK47.

The one with the AK held his hand up while the shotgun carrier covered them.

'Wait. Leave you weapons out here.'

'Your mother,' countered Petrus.

'No one sees Fat Man armed.'

'I do.'

The man shook his head.

'Right,' said Petrus. 'We can do this one of two ways, one, go and ask Fat Man or, two, I'll just go in, you'll try to stop me and then Fat Man sends someone to look for some new bodyguards.'

Garrett surreptitiously slipped the safety off the CR-21. But the sound was louder than he thought and both sets of bodyguard's eyes swiveled nervously towards him.

'Okay,' said the bodyguard with the AK. 'Wait and I'll ask. Stand there.'

He opened the door and stuck his head around. There was a hurried conversation, sotto voce. He pulled his head back, looking sheepish. 'Sorry, mister

Dlamini, sir. I didn't know that it was you. Please go in.'

Petrus went in first followed by Garrett. The bodyguards stayed outside.

The room wasn't large. It had been converted from three, single room apartments; all the walls taken down to provide one open plan area. The windows had been bricked up, leaving only small slits. Gun ports.

A seventy-two-inch plasma television graced the one wall and the lighting was provided from at least twenty lava-lamps in red and blue. The furniture all black leather and chrome. A bad 1960s sci-fi set.

And seated on the one double sofa was the biggest man that Garrett had ever seen. Perhaps slightly over normal height but his breadth took up the entire sofa. Garrett estimated him to be North of 700 pounds. It was obvious why he was called Fat Man.

He stood up off the sofa and walked towards Petrus, his arms out. They met and Fat Man gave Petrus a huge bear hug. He made the six feet two-hundred-pound warrior look like an emaciated child.

Petrus introduced him. Fat man, this is Garrett. A good friend. Garrett, Fat Man.'

Fat Man shook Garrett's hand.

'Hello, friend of Petrus,' he said. His voice was light and high. Almost falsetto. A seven-hundred-pound Michael Jackson. 'So, come. Sit down. Tell me what's happening.'

They arranged themselves on the leather sofas. Now that Garrett was closer, he could see that the Fat Man's sofa had been reinforced with two-inch rolled steel joists, welded together and then bolted to the original frame. Even so, the entire structure flexed and groaned when he sat down.

'You guys hungry?' He asked. 'I'm getting some chow in, I'll get extra.'

Petrus nodded. 'Thanks, Fat Man.'

Fat Man gestured to Garrett. 'Friend of Petrus, call one of the doormen in, please.'

Garrett went to the door, opened it and asked one of the guards to come in.

'Ah, Chester. Send some boys to get take away. Kentucky fried chicken. Tell them, five family feast buckets, ten extra fries, ten tubs of coleslaw and ketchup.' He turned to Petrus. 'You like fried chicken?'

Petrus nodded.

'Okay, make that seven family feast buckets and twenty fries. There's cash on the table there,' he pointed at a coffee table next to the door. The guard grabbed a handful of notes and left, closing the door behind him.

'Talk to me, Petrus.'

So, Petrus gave the Fat Man an abbreviated run down on the last few days events, ending with that fact that the police force was now after them – although they were buggered if they knew why.

As Petrus finished his tale there was a knock on the door and two of the young men from the lobby walked in laden down with buckets of chicken and fries and large bottles of green soda of some type. They lay them out on the low table that was in front of the Fat Man's sofa.

'So,' said the Fat Man. 'You have already met my lost boys.'

Petrus nodded.

The Fat Man chuckled. 'They seek to be American street thugs. Niggas. All bling and bullshit, but they're good boys. Faithful.' He rubbed one on the head. A pet dog.

They left and closed the door behind them.

The Fat Man tore open a bucket of chicken and started eating. It was plain to Garrett and Petrus that conversation was over until consumption had finished so they took a bucket each and ate as well, swilling it down with super-sweet mouthfuls of the virulent green pop.

Fat Man ate like a man driven by exterior forces. An automaton. Chicken flesh was stripped neatly off the bone to be ingested and fries were bundled, dipped in ketchup and thrust in after. He was neat. He spilt neither crumbs nor fat, stopping every now and then to pat his lips delicately with a paper napkin. In the same time that Garrett had eaten two pieces of chicken, Fat Man had polished off a family bucket of twelve pieces and was starting to get into his stride, working two handed. One shuttling the chicken back and forth and the other bundling, dipping and inserting handfuls of fries. It was like watching a well-engineered machine at work. Silent, efficient and impressive.

Within twenty minutes Fat Man had finished all. He opened a half gallon bottle of the green soda, put it to his lips and downed it without taking breath. Then he burped mightily, patted his stomach and continued the conversation as if they had not paused.

'Right, you guys can stay here in the hostel for a while. I'll get my boys to try and find out what's going down with the cops. But I tell you, Petrus, this doesn't sound good. I'm not a conspiracy nut but this smacks of some sort of plot.' He pointed at Garrett. 'Please ask one of the guards to come in.'

Garrett stood up, opened the door and asked a guard to come on.

'Sampson,' said Fat Man. 'Take Petrus and his friend, find them a room. They can use one of the rooms where the people are working night shift. Okay, guys, I'll see you in the morning.'

Garrett and Petrus followed Sampson from the room. They walked down the corridor and across the lobby to a set of stairs. They went up the stairs to the next floor. Another long, badly lit corridor. Half way down Sampson stopped and opened a door.

'Here. This room is empty tonight. The occupants are working nightshift at the city morgue. Sleep here.' He turned and left without another word.

The room was small. Two iron beds, covered in rough gray blankets. A stainless steel sink. Plywood cupboard with a broken door. The floor was bare concrete polished to a shine with red floor wax. The light, a dirty forty-watt bulb. A window, steel bars.

Garrett sat down on one of the beds. The bedding stank of old sweat. Rancid. Sour. The threadbare pillow was shiny with grease. There was a spot of dried blood on the blanket. He didn't care. He had slept in places far worse. And he was tired. He took his jacket off and spread it over the pillow and then lay down on top of the blanket, fully dressed.

'Good night, Petrus.'

'Night.'

Within minutes the two were asleep.

***

Pete and four of his men had spent the night sleeping in the offices of Phoenix Building Supplies. Today was Sunday so the premises were deserted.

Isaac had given them a set of keys as well as the weapons and ammunition. He had explained the situation regarding Petrus and then he had left.

After coffee Pete got the men together in the main office and led them in Sunday prayers. He thanked the Lord for the opportunity that they had and asked for his help in finding the Zulu and capturing him alive. He also thanked the Lord for their unknown benefactor and the guns and ammunition. Finally, he asked that the lord guide them and help them to a new white homeland.

All five of the Afrikaners were dressed in shabby jeans, dark shirts and sneakers. On their heads, covering their hair, were knitted watch caps, pulled down low. They had all used black camouflage cream to darken their faces and hands a uniform black. This would prevent them standing out as a group of white boys in the Alexandra Township. All wore long coats to conceal their assault rifles.

They were good to go.

***

The four-seater Eurocopter MBB BO105 hammered through the early morning air. The pilot and gunner sat in the front two seats. In the back seat was sergeant Fumba. In the fourth seat was a cardboard box. It was full of printed leaflets. A5 size. On them a simple message printed in English, Afrikaans, Zulu and Xhosa.

WANTED – ALIVE.

Petrus Dlamini

REWARD – R200 000

Fumba pointed at the hostel. 'Start there, that's the Zulu controlled area. That's where they'll be.'

The pilot took the helicopter over the hostel and slowed down. Sergeant Fumba grabbed a handful of leaflets and chucked them out of the open side door. The downdraft snatched at them and scattered them like giant snowflakes.

'Go back around,' said Fumba. 'I'll throw some more out.'

'Be quick,' shouted the pilot. 'If we hang about in one place too long the Zulus start shooting at us.'

'Why?' Asked Fumba.

The pilot shrugged. 'No reason Just for fun.'

They turned and did another pass. More leaflets filled the skies. Then the pilot took the machine in a slow circle around the township. Fumba threw out leaflets until the box was empty and they left, heading East towards the police heliport.

Meanwhile, on the ground, colonel Zuzani had called in a long list of favors and now had, under his direct command, two hundred and fifty well-armed policemen and six Casspir armored cars.

He had used the two hundred new men to completely cordon off the Alexandra Township. Every outgoing road had been blockaded and all major roads had one of the Casspirs to provide armored support.

This show of force combined with the cash reward made Zuzani certain that someone would bring in Dlamini very soon. The whole operation should be over in a couple of hours, if not sooner.

***

Garrett sat on the edge of the bed and used his fingers to shovel the stiff boiled maize meal porridge into his mouth. One of the lost boys had brought the porridge and two mugs of industrial strength coffee with at least five spoons of sugar in.

As they were finishing, they heard a helicopter clatter over them, flying low and slow. Minutes later one of the lost boys rushed into the room.

'Fat Man wants to see you. Now.'

The two of them grabbed their weapons and followed the lost boy to Fat Man's rooms.

Fat Man was sitting on his leather sofa. The place looked the same. Blue and red from the myriad of bubbling lava lamps. The fried chicken buckets had been cleared away and in their place was a mountain of egg McMuffins. Garrett guessed at maybe forty. Maybe fifty. Next to them a few gallons of the ubiquitous green soda.

'Come in,' he said. 'Sit. Eat.'

Petrus shook his head. 'Just eaten, thanks.'

The Fat Man downed a huge draft of green fizzy liquid straight from the bottle and then ate a few more McMuffins. He would put a whole one in his mouth at once and then chew stolidly. A set look of concentration his face. Each one went down in under ten seconds. An industrial McMuffin disposal unit.

He lent forward and grabbed a handful of leaflets. Threw them at Petrus.

'Check this out. This is big shit, man. Big shit.'

Petrus scanned one of the papers. 'Two hundred grand. It's a fucking insult. Back in the day, the apartheid government had a price of five hundred K on my head, dead or alive.'

The Fat Man laughed. High pitched. Feminine. 'Maybe so, but you know what it costs to hire a hit on someone nowadays?'

Petrus shrugged.

'Two grand. Two thousand lousy Rands. Two hundred dollars American for a life. Two hundred grand is four year's salary for a street hit man. They are going to come crawling out of the fucking woodwork. Armies of the fuckers. Big shit.'

'What do you suggest?' asked Petrus.

The Fat Man ingested a few more egg McMuffins while he thought. His jaws ruminating like a cow chewing the cud.

'What would happen if you died and your father found out that I might have been able to prevent it?'

It was not a rhetorical question so Petrus gave it some thought before answering.

'He would consider it an insult. He would rally his shields to him, put them on buses and come here to chastise you.'

'How many?'

Petrus laughed. 'All of them. He would raze this place to the ground.'

Fat Man sighed. 'Petrus, I want you to know, I would help you anyway but it's not as though I have any choice in the matter. You are the son of my chief. I will do all that I can, as will my people.'

Petrus bowed his head in thanks.

'You,' Fat Man gestured at Garrett. 'Call a guard.'

Garrett opened the door and summoned Sampson.

'Sampson,' said the Fat Man. 'Take the lost boys, start here in the hostel and then work the streets. Show them these leaflets and tell everyone that if we even see someone holding one, we will kill them and their family. Make examples. Okay?'

Sampson nodded. 'I will need more people; there are only ten lost boys. I need another ten men.'

The Fat Man waved his hand. 'Take. Whatever. Start now.'

'That should sort things out,' said Garrett.

The Fat Man shook his head. 'No. It will stop any of the Zulus from running you in, but my influence dwindles the further one goes from the hostel. The Xhosas control the other side of Alex. They will use this as an excuse to attack us.' He rammed another McMuffin down. Chewed. 'This is the beginning of a war. Bad shit. Very bad.'

Petrus stood up. 'We can take them, Fat Man. We can take them.'

The Fat Man shrugged. 'Probably. But last time we had a war they burned down the McDonalds. I had to have fried chicken for breakfast until they rebuilt. I hate having chicken for breakfast. It just isn't right.' He picked up a bottle of green soda, took a gulp and stood up. 'Right, gentlemen. Let's prepare for battle.'

Her real name was Mary Morgan. She hated it. But she liked the initials. MM. Like the candy. It had a hook. So, she kept the initials and called herself Misty Malone.

Misty had worked her way up from local cable weather to state cable weather. She was good at her job. Five seven, blonde, blue eyed with a figure that is seldom seen in reality. But she didn't want to be a weather girl. Even the name was a denigration. Channels had weather *men,* not weather boys, so why girls?

Misty wanted to do serious news. She wanted to be a political correspondent. So, while she had been chirping away every day about the sun, sun, sun in California, she had also been taking night classes in political economy through Cornell University and she had graduated in the top five percent of her class.

And, because she worked hard and was good at her job. And also, because the gods of television are a cruel bunch, Misty got her wish and was promoted to the position of Foreign Correspondent, Southern Africa Division. What this meant is that she had been sent on a three-month mission to South Africa. The company had booked her into the Gauteng, Sandton Holiday Inn Plaza, outside Johannesburg and they had hired her a part-time cameraman. A forty-five-year-old Afrikaner called Bartholomew. Street smart and tough as nails, he was her guide and assistant as well as cameraman.

Misty had now been in South Africa for three weeks now and she had worked hard. But none of her material had been used. The simple fact of the matter was; no one cared any more. The days of South Africa being news were long gone. Nelson Mandela was on his deathbed. The political set up had become yet another African caricature of itself, fraught with endemic corruption and nepotism. The endless hi-jackings, rapes and murders were bad, but America had its own surfeit of those crimes so, although the actual preponderance might have been news, the crimes themselves were not.

Misty knew that unless she got some real story, something with some meat to it, when she flew back home it would be to a severance check, a pat on the back and a curt goodbye. Television had no time for losers.

And then her cell rang. It was Bartholomew.

'Howzit, Misty?' He greeted her with the standard South African shortening of the phrase, how is it going. He continued without waiting for an answer. 'Listen, girl, there's some weird shit going down in the Alexandra Township. The cops have cordoned off the whole area and there's helicopters dropping leaflets. I'm on my way to you. We need to get down there.'

He disconnected before Misty could answer.

She grabbed her travel bag with her microphone, makeup and money and headed for the hotel lobby.

***

Pete and his four men were in Alexandra. They had pierced the police cordon with ease, ghosting past them before sun up. Quiet and deadly.

But they were in very unfamiliar surroundings. Instead of the fresh open farmland that they had trained in, there was cramped squalor. Tin shacks placed so close together that their shoulders brushed on each side as they walked.

Pete spoke five African languages fluently so he was not worried about finding Petrus. It was simply police work, albeit in a slightly different guise. Knock on enough doors, ask enough questions and, in time, you would get the answers.

Pete did not know which area of Alexandra the Zulus, or Xhosas or Sothos or Tsongas controlled. He also did not fully appreciate that, with almost three quarters of a million people jammed into the area, nothing could be done quickly. The simple magnitude of the task would ensure that it took time.

He pushed the door of the first shack open and stepped inside while his men stood guard.

A mother and two children were crouched in the corner of the tiny room. Dirt floor, no windows. Some threadbare blankets piled on a square of plastic sheeting. They stared at the huge, armed white man in terror. Eyes opened impossibly wide.

'I am looking for the Zulu, Petrus Dlamini. Do you know him?' Asked Pete.

The children whimpered and the mother shook her head.

'Are you sure?' asked Pete again.

There was no answer. The mother was now shaking with fear. Pete turned on his heel and left. Onto the next shack.

It was empty. The next had a whole family inside. Father, mother, three children. If they all lay down at the same time, they would fill the floor space wall to wall. Pete asked the same question. The father answered.

'There are no Zulus here. This area is Xhosa controlled. If there were any Zulus here, they would be dead ones.'

Pete frowned. 'What do you mean?'

'The Zulus live that side,' the man pointed. 'By the Madala hostel. They don't come here and we don't go there. If people here see strangers, then they shoot at them. There are snipers in all of the tall buildings.'

Pete backed out of the shack. His men were waiting for him. One of them stepped forward; he had a piece of paper in his hand.

'*Kommandant*, you need to see this. I found it on the ground. There's lots of them.' He handed the leaflet to Pete who scanned it quickly. It was one of the reward notices. He shook his head.

'What the fuck is going on here? Who the hell did this? Who else is looking for the Zulu?'

He felt a momentary flutter of panic. Things were starting to unravel. Without Petrus there would be no arms cache. Without the arms cache there would be no possibility of military action. And without that, his dream of a white homeland would be gone forever. And now someone else was looking for Petrus.

'Right, boys. We need to find the Zulu before any-one else does. Let's get to it. We need to go that way,' he pointed in the direction that the shack dweller had said.

The group set off at a jog. Pete in front and the four others running two abreast behind him.

As they started to run the air was rent with the sound of a high velocity rifle and one of Pete's men fell to the ground. The rest of them went down and scuttled close to the shacks.

Pete grabbed his fallen man by his collar and dragged him into cover. He had been hit in the chest. It looked like a .308 round. Standard hunting rifle. He would have been dead before he hit the ground. Pete scanned the area. In the distance was a row of four-story apartments. The walls streaked with filth and smoke stains. Windows broken and boarded over. The shot must have come from there. They had obviously stood out as strangers, regardless of their blackened faces and attire, the assault rifles were new generation and would be noticed. Pete wished that they had been given AK47s, but beggars can't be choosers.

He glanced across at his boys. They looked nervous. Quick of breath and shaking slightly. Pete didn't mind. That was normal. It was their first real contact. He had chosen his best and now, he hoped, they would prove his choice correct.

'Listen up, boys,' he said. 'Garvey is dead. Nothing that we can do. We're exposed out here. We'll come back for him later. Be very wary. Eyes open, there's more than snipers out there, this place is crawling with uglies and there's someone else looking for Dlamini as well. We don't know if they're friendly or not so stay cool. What we need to do now is head towards the Zulu controlled area and find Dlamini. The best way to do that is to go straight through these fucking shacks. Follow me.'

Pete kicked the door to the nearest shack open and barreled in. His three men sprinted across the lane and followed. A bullet kicked up dust behind them as another round was fired at them.

Four people huddled in the corner. The whites of their eyes showing in wide eyed terror. Pete raised his foot to his chest and simply booted out the back wall. They all ran through into the adjoining shack. Two occupants who took one look at the weapons and simply lay on the floor. Inert. Pete ignored them, kicked their sidewall out and kept going.

Four shacks and less than a minute later they were out of the killing zone. Blocked off from the sniper's position. Pete called for a rest.

*****

Fat Man moved like the behemoth he was. A slow and implacable force of nature.

His people loved him. He knew all by name and asked after family members and friends. He patted people on the back or playfully punched shoulders. But at all times he radiated an aura of leadership. He was friendly, but not a friend. He was their leader.

He sent two snipers onto the roof, then he had put two gunmen in each ground floor room. One in each of the rooms on the second floor. Women and children had been relegated to the third floor. His men were armed with a selection of AKs, hunting rifles, shotguns and sidearms. There seemed to be plenty of ammunition.

The lost boys had congregated in the lobby, their reinforcement mission amongst the locals completed successfully. Garrett had a chance to look at them again and he took back his initial thought that they were a bunch of clowns. Now that action was in the offing, he could see past their bling and their bullshit. There was no nervousness. No false bravado. Their eyes were cold and calculating. They were at ease. Ready to fight. He could see why they were Fat Man's chosen disciples.

Garrett took Petrus aside. 'Is this for real?' He asked. 'I mean, are we seriously talking a war here?'

Petrus nodded. 'Things have been on the verge of sparking off for a while now. This has just provided the excuse that everyone was looking for.'

'But won't the cops come in? Or the army?'

Petrus laughed. Genuine amusement. 'No way, man. The cops would get slaughtered and no one wants to send the army in. Too much like the old apartheid days. Wouldn't make political sense. No, they'll just let us fight it out. It's happened before and it'll happen again.'

Garrett nodded and went outside. Stood in front of the doors to the hostel. Looked across the shacks. The sun had risen. Groups of people were walking to work. Children played in the streets and the filth. A lot of people simply sat in the doorways to their rudimentary shelters. Listless. No jobs. No life. Nothing.

A mere two miles away was one of the most expensive suburbs on the African continent. A suburb where one had to be a multimillionaire simply to buy the cheapest house let alone live the extravagant lifestyle that such an address demanded.

Garrett had fought wars in Eritrea where he had seen innocent villages napalmed back to the Stone

Age. He had fought in Rwanda where ethnic cleansing had taken place on both sides. Burundi. Uganda. Somalia. Djibouti. But he had never before seen such dire third world poverty living unchecked right next to such extravagant first world luxury.

He lit a cigarette, leaning his assault rifle against the wall as he did so. In the distance he heard a rifle shot. A few seconds later a second one. Large caliber. There was no return fire. Sniper at work.

One of the lost boys came out of the building and stood next to him. Garrett took his pack out and offered.

He accepted. Lit himself, his Zippo appearing in his hand as if by magic. One handed. A move that had taken a lot of practice.

'They will come tonight,' he said. 'Never in the day.'

'How many?' Asked Garrett.

The lost boy shrugged. 'Not many. They will test. Maybe some grenades. Petrol bombs. The next night there will be more.'

'How do you know?'

'It is always such.'

'Why don't we attack them?'

The lost boy shook his head. 'Fat Man doesn't attack. He believes that we should all live in peace. If they attack, we fight back. Seldom do we have retaliatory raids.'

'Do you agree with Fat Man?'

'It doesn't matter.'

'But if you had a choice,' Garrett continued.

'If I had a choice,' the lost boy ground his cigarette out beneath his sneaker. 'If I had a choice, I would burn this whole fucking township to the ground.' He turned and walked back into the hostel.

Garrett lit another cigarette. He sensed more than heard Petrus walk up behind him.

'You know, *isosha*,' Petrus said. 'A couple of years ago the people here decided that the reason that their lives were so shit was because the foreigners, Zimbabweans and such what, were taking their jobs. So, they got together and killed about fifty of them. They killed them during the day. During the week. Nobody thought to ask, if these guys are taking our jobs, then why are they sitting here in this shithole with us instead of being at work. A few months after that a car drove past a church gathering and opened fire on the congregation. Killed twenty people, mostly women and children. A reprisal from the foreigners. If someone who looks like they don't belong walks to close to any of the hostels then a sniper takes them out. Officially there are around twenty or thirty reported deaths a day here. In reality it's probably five times that.'

Garrett dragged on his cigarette. 'Yeah, I get it. It's a shit place to live.'

'No, my friend. The reason that I'm telling you this is because I know you well. I know the way that you think. You're standing here, right now thinking; this upcoming war is our fault. If Petrus and I weren't here then everything would be fine. Well, bullshit. Here, not here, doesn't matter. These dudes kill each other all the time. It's just what they do. Not our fault. Anyway, where would you go? There's a countrywide APB out on you. You can't go to any airports or cross the border. You move outside of Alex and they'll get you. So, my friend, this is it.'

The two stood together and watched the township live and breathe. A huge misery-driven monster. A cancer on the face of humanity.

CHAPTER TWENTY-SIX

Some people knew his real name. Others claimed to, but they were being less than liberal with the truth.

But whatever it was, everyone called him Mister Clean. And in the Xhosa controlled sector of Alexandra; Mister Clean was the law.

If someone were asked to describe Mister Clean it would prove to be a task that was at once very easy and, at the same time, impossible to achieve with any semblance of accuracy. You see, Mister Clean was average. Five foot ten, not fat but not thin. Hair, cut shortish, by a mid-range gentleman's barber. An adequately fitted suit brought off the peg from a middle of the market chain store.

Average.

Until you looked into his eyes. That was like staring into dark, shark infested waters. It was the abyss staring back at you.

Unlike Fat Man's disco-themed chrome and leather control room, Mister Clean favored a classroom environment. He sat at the front behind a moderately priced wooden desk and his eight lieutenants sat arrayed before him on lecture chairs with small writing desks attached. He didn't go so far as to have a chalkboard on the wall but he did issue each lieutenant with a clipboard and a notebook. On each clipboard was one of the leaflets that sergeant Fumba had dropped that morning.

Mister Clean held up a copy for all to see. 'Two hundred thousand Rands, gentlemen. We want that money.'

There was a chorus of agreement.

'As well as the money, we would also love to see that Dlamini taken away, never to be seen again.'

Another chorus of affirmation. This one even stronger than the first. Petrus was well known and well hated by the men sitting in Mister Cleans control room.

Mister Clean pointed at one of the lieutenants. 'Bambata, go to Jama's room, he has the hand grenades. Get three from him. Then take two men with AK's. I want you to get as close as you can to the Zulu hostel. We always attack at night so this time we go in the afternoon, they won't expect it. There will be people hanging around outside the front door. Use the grenades. Try to get one into the lobby. Shoot anyone still standing and then get out. Can you do that?'

'Yes, sir.'

'Good. Now go. The rest of you, take your men and form a perimeter, from 17th street to Selbourne Avenue.'

The men left to follow Mister Clean's orders. He sat behind his desk for a while and thought. This was his chance. His chance to deal the Zulu contingent a savage blow and drive them from Alexandra. Send them back to KwaZulu where they came from. Mister Clean hated the Zulus. Not for some xenophobic reason couched in the rehashing of past sins. He hated them because of their arrogance and bloody mindedness. For the fact that they held themselves apart from the rest of South Africans with their own king and their own command structure. Mister Clean was convinced that the failure of the new South Africa to provide for its people was purely and simply the fault of the arrogant Zulu nation and he would not rest until they had been defeated. And now he had been provided with an excellent opportunity.

He stood up from his chair and went to see that his lieutenants were doing his bidding.

✻✻✻

Bartholomew picked Misty up from outside the Holiday Inn and driven to the outskirts of Alexandra. They parked some distance from one of the major roadblocks, Misty checked her makeup, Bart powered up his camera and they stepped out of the car.

Misty passed her eyes over the group of policemen. There were at least thirty of them. Most in full combat gear, R4 assault rifles, pistols, steel and Kevlar armor and helmets. But two stood apart, dressed in tailored combat fatigues. One had a pistol in a shoulder holster. The other appeared unarmed, on his shoulder epaulettes a subtle two stars and a castle. Misty had memorized her ranks. She approached him.

'Excuse me, colonel, Misty Malone CBT Cable, may we talk?'

The man walked up to Misty and held out his hand. Misty took it and they shook. His grip was firm but not overpowering. His skin cool and dry. But she could feel ridges and calluses, both on his palm and his knuckles. This was no desk jockey's hand. This was the feel of a man who had used his hands for physical work. And violence.

'Good day, Misty. I am colonel Gideon Zuzani. Please, call me Gideon,' Zuzani smiled, his teeth were Hollywood perfect and when he grinned his eyes crinkled slightly at the corners. As if he was sharing a private joke with you. The sheer strength of his charisma and sexuality almost took Misty's breath away. He radiated a palpable aura of confidence and power and she felt herself blush, hating herself for it even as it was happening.

But she was a professional and she rallied quickly. 'Thank you, Gideon.' She gestured to Bart who shouldered his camera. 'So, Gideon, could you tell us exactly what is going on here today?'

'Of course, Misty. It's nothing to get excited about, simply a joint exercise involving several different departments of the police force. The army has their war games and we have this.' He smiled.

'And what about the helicopter dropping leaflets, Gideon. What was that all about?'

'That was simply a notice to the residents of Alexandra telling them of the exercise and keeping them in the loop so that no one panicked. Misty, I am sorry that I couldn't give you a more interesting story but, unfortunately, there's nothing more to tell.' Again, the Hollywood smile.

At the same time there was a rattle of automatic gunfire followed by a huge explosion in the middle of the township. This was followed by more gunfire. A pall of smoke rose into the still afternoon air.

Misty raised an eyebrow. 'Colonel, I think that perhaps we should start this interview again,' she said.

***

Bambata strode through the narrow passageway between the two rows of shacks. Behind him were two of his men. All three carried AK47s. Bambata was weighed down a little further as he had three hand grenades in his jacket pockets.

They made no attempt at stealth as they were, as yet, still far from the Zulu controlled area and so they walked with attitude. This was their end of town and they demanded respect.

At the end of the passageway, they turned right, into another corrugated steel canyon of shacks. And standing there, facing them, were four men. The first thing that Bambata noticed was that they were holding some sort of new generation assault rifle that he hadn't seen before. The second thing that he noticed was, although they appeared to have black skin - they were not black.

Both groups looked at each other for almost a full second. Bambata reacted first, whipping up his AK and pulling the trigger. The weapon was set to full auto and, as a result, it kicked high and to the right, climbing above the other group's heads.

Three of the men in the other group dove for cover. But the leader stood firm, and fired a quick double-tap at Bambata. Both rounds hit him high on his left shoulder, spinning him to the ground. He rolled to the side, behind a forty-four-gallon drum of water. Behind him his two men had gone to ground and were returning fire.

But the leader of the opposite group calmly adjusted his aim and double-tapped both of them through the tops of their heads. Bambata was hyperventilating with fear. His lungs pumping surplus oxygen through his system much faster than he could use it. There was nothing left to do, he pulled a grenade from his pocket, ripped out the pin and threw it.

Pete watched the grenade sail through the air towards him. His internal battle-clock started to count down. He had heard the spoon fly off the grenade. He could see that it was an old Portuguese M312. He did not panic because he knew that it had a burn time of 5 – 7 seconds. He caught it with one hand, flicked it back and dropped to the ground. It exploded about three feet above Bambata's head, killing him instantly and throwing up a cloud of dust and smoke. This was clearly both seen and heard by Misty Malone who was busy interviewing colonel Zuzani.

Pete motioned to his men and they set off at a sprint, taking whatever turn came to fancy. Losing themselves in the jigsaw of broken dwellings. After ten minutes they ducked into a shack. Amazingly, it was empty. Most probably the occupants had already fled from the gunfire.

'Bakkies,' said Pete to the one man. 'Keep watch at the door. Is everyone alright?'

There was a smattering of agreement.

Pete sat down on the floor, pulled a pack from his shirt pocket and lit up. 'Fuck me, this place is a mad house. Listen, boys. We're going to hole up here until sundown. Go in under cover of night. Rest. Bakkies, first watch. Victor, an hour from now. Stephan, after that. Anything, and I mean anything worries you, wake me.'

***

Mister Clean was upset. But he didn't show it. That would be unseemly. Childish. But the fact that the Zulus had somehow outmaneuvered him hurt him to the quick. How had they known that he had sent his men out early? How had they known where they were? And how had they dispatched them so easily? He knew Bambata well and he was no pushover, but the fact of the matter is, Bambata and his men were dead. Taken out with ease and with no corresponding cost of life from the enemy.

But then Petrus Dlamini was known to be a warrior of note. And the word on the street was that his white foreign friend was even better than Petrus himself. Mister Clean chastised himself. He had been overconfident. He had underestimated his foe. Well, no more. He left his room to collect his lieutenants. This time he would do things properly. This time he would go himself.

***

'Two groups,' said Garrett. 'One with AK's, the other, M16s or some other 5.56mm weapon.'

Petrus accepted his friends comment without question. 'A skirmish, gang members perhaps?' He asked.

Garrett shook his head. 'One of the groups is military. Well trained. Maybe even Special Forces. Three sets of double taps. Controlled. The other group simply fired on full auto. Amateurs.'

'The explosion?'

'Grenade,' answered Garrett. 'Old. Slow burn. Deep thud as opposed to the crack of the new grenades.'

'So,' said Petrus. 'Who?'

Garrett shrugged. 'How should I know? This is your patch, you tell me.'

'Maybe we should go and take a look.'

Garrett shook his head. 'Not me. I don't like it at all. Some random detachment of Special Forces dudes running around, other dudes with hand grenades. No way. Let's stay here, see what else goes down. Maybe nighttime we go out. Maybe.'

***

Colonel Zuzani stared at the plume of smoke for a while. When he turned to face Misty, the smile had gone from his face. In its place was an expression carved from granite. Cold. Overbearing.

'This interview is over,' he said. 'There is nothing of interest here.'

'But colonel,' insisted Misty. 'What about…'

Zuzani snapped his fingers, and sergeant Fumba trotted over.

'Sergeant, remove these people. Escort them to the end of the road. Take five men with you and ensure that no one else comes down. Especially no press members. If anyone causes any trouble, charge them with perverting the course of justice and take them to the Wynberg police cells. Go.'

Fumba pulled his pistol from his shoulder holster. 'Okay, people. Let's move. Now.' He used the firearm to gesture towards Bart's car.

Misty was about to argue but Bart grabbed her arm and shook his head. 'Don't even think about it,' he whispered. 'Come, let's go.'

Bart opened the door for Misty, chucked his camera on the back seat, scuttled around to the driver's side and got in. He cranked the engine to life and drove off.

'The bastard,' said Misty. 'What the hell is going on there?'

Bart shrugged.

'Well, whatever it is,' said Misty. 'We are going back tonight and we are going to find out.'

'Oh shit,' said Bart. 'That's all I need. Great. An evening in hell with an over ambitious weather girl.'

'Bart.'

'Ja.'

'Fuck you.'

Bart laughed.

CHAPTER TWENTY-SEVEN

Manhattan threw up into the basin. It burned his throat. Hot and acidic. Like live coals. It had seemed so simple. The kidnapping had gone well. Keeping his identity and the true plan secret from Pete Vermulen had gone well. Raising the one hundred million dollars had been difficult, but not insurmountable.

And now it was unraveling faster than a thrift store jersey. He was two days away from losing everything. His money, his estates. His standing in society. Everything. All because of Petrus Dlamini and his white pet. He heaved again, but his stomach was empty. A tiny string of bile dropped from his lips. His wiped it off with the back of his hand. Stood for a while.

Then he washed his face and walked back out into the world.

***

Garrett had sat outside all day and now he watched the sun sink below the horizon. The thick layers of pollution bent its rays into a collage of reds and purples as it slowly died its daily death.

And the township started to change. From a bad dream to a nightmare.

Small fires were being lit everywhere. For cooking, for warmth and for light. Wood, cardboard, plastic and rubber. Smoke boiled from the myriad of personal flames. Dark and choking it covered the land like a plague. Within half an hour it was as thick as an old London pea souper. Visibility cut to ten yards at most.

People trudged through the haze, coming back from their long, underpaid jobs. Clutching small packets of food to their breasts. Children waited stoically, knowing that cries of hunger made no difference. Those who had little shared with those who had none.

And all around the township, men with weapons made themselves ready. For tonight the killing would begin.

In the hostel were Fat Man's people. The snipers useless in the current miasma of smoke.

In the center of the township, waiting, sat The Prophet and his three men.

And in the Xhosa controlled area Mister Clean stood in front of thirty of his men. They were armed with a mix of AKs, shotguns, rifles, sidearms and hand grenades. They also all carried petrol bombs. Simple half gallon glass bottles filled with a mixture of gas and oil. In the neck a fuel-soaked rag.

His plan was simple. They would break into three groups of ten with him leading one of the groups. The one group would drive through the middle of the township and the others would advance on either flank. At ten o'clock they would fall on the Zulu hostel like a rain of fire, getting as close as possible and attempting to get as many of the Molotov Cocktails into the actual building as possible. They would then dispatch anyone running from the building. This was to be the end of Zulu supremacy in Alexandra.

***

And sitting in a car in a suburb on the outskirts of Alexandra sat a South African cameraman and a reporter from America.

'You look ridiculous,' said Bart.

'It's camouflage,' retorted Misty.

'Bullshit. It's what camouflage would look like if Barbie put it on. You're meant to cover your whole face with camo. Not a few subtle streaks of green and black.'

'Bart, stop being so dense, will you? It's not meant to be real; it's meant to look combat-chique. It's for the camera.'

'Oh, well then it looks good. Quite sexy. I like that black catsuit.'

'Excellent,' said Misty. 'Right then, let's go.'

The both got out of the car, locked it and began walking to Alexandra, keeping in the shadows. Hugging the hedges.

As they got closer the smoke started to get heavier.

'Jesus,' said Misty. 'What's this? Is this normal?'

'Smoke from their fires. Thousands of fires. There's not much electricity so they rely on flame for cooking, warmth, seeing. Company.'

'But why does it smell so rank?'

'Not a lot of wood around,' answered Bart. 'So, they tend to burn anything that's flammable. A lot of plastic and industrial waste. Paint, old engine oil, shit like that.'

'It burns your throat.'

'Breath shallow,' advised Bart. 'It gets a lot worse.'

They walked for a while longer. After ten minutes they were on the outskirts of Alex, hidden in the smoke.

'Now listen, Misty,' said Bart. 'Follow me. Do what I do. I'm being serious now. This is going to be scary; you haven't had any combat reporting experience so prepare yourself. No screaming if you get a fright, it'll give away our position. Also, if we get caught by someone, let me do the talking, okay?'

Misty flicked her hair. 'Don't be so paranoid, Bart. We're members of the press, they won't harm us.'

Bart stopped walking. 'Misty, just stop. These guys don't give a shit about the press. They're not some bunch of MTV teenagers looking to be on TV. These guys have been brought up in a war zone. They are the most unpredictable mother-fuckers you will ever meet. They might ignore you; they might talk to you. They might shoot you, rape you. Cut you up. Please, if you don't agree to listen to me then I am out of here.'

Misty stared at Bart for a while. 'You scared?'

Bart nodded. 'Petrified.'

Mist was taken aback. Bart was fearless. They had covered car accidents, muggings, robberies. They had been threatened by policemen and thugs and he had never even blinked. But now he had admitted to his own fear Misty's heart had started hammering against her rib cage like a bird with a broken wing.

She nodded; her face serious. 'Okay, Bartholomew. I'll listen.'

'Good.'

They entered Alex by climbing over a wooden fence into someone's tiny patch of dirt they called a garden. Avoiding the police.

'Okay, Bart,' said Misty. 'Do me.'

Bart thumbed on his camera and adjusted the focus, centering Misty.

She looked directly into the lens, her hair framing her camo-chique face perfectly. A modern-day Joan of Arc.

'After this afternoon's aborted interview with colonel Zuzani of the South African Police Force I decided to delve further into what is happening in the Alexandra Township, outside Gauteng, South Africa. Why has the entire township been shut down by the police? Why were they dropping leaflets to the township dwellers? What were the explosions and the gunfire that we heard earlier on today? Even in an area as violent as this, this type of behavior is highly unusual. So, I have sneaked in, under cover of darkness, to get to the bottom of this mystery and, regardless of the danger that I might find myself in, I will get to the truth. This is Misty Malone for CBT Cable.'

Bart gave a thumbs up and switched off.

'Great,' he said. 'What now?'

Misty shrugged. 'Not sure. I suppose that we simply sneak around and see what we can pick up.'

'Okay,' agreed Bart. 'Works for me. Let's sneak.'

They edged around the side of the shack and proceeded to slink down the lane, disappearing into the acrid smoke.

***

Pete gestured to his three men and ducked outside the shack. They followed him in single file. He squinted through the smoke. He could see people through the open sides of their shacks. Eating. Sitting. Talking in low voices. As if fearful that someone would overhear them.

In the 1980s during the apartheid era, Pete had spent a lot of time in townships. But never in Alex, always in

SOWETO or one of the bigger, well-lit townships. This was totally different. After he had taken two or three turns, he was completely lost. There were no discernable landmarks. Passageways ended in dead ends or circled back on themselves. Some of the roads were blocked with barricades of broken cars, rusting steel bed frames and burnt out forty-gallon drums.

Pete stopped, holding up his hand so that his men followed his example. He waved at them and they went down on one knee, rifles at their shoulders ready to fire. He scanned the vista around him. He couldn't get a bearing on the stars due to the smoke. The lights from Sandton were similarly diffuse for the same reasons. He peered through a gap between two of the shacks. It looked like there was a tarred road through there.

He crooked a finger at his men, squeezed through the gap and they followed.

They came out onto a narrow, potholed road. No pavement. Shacks built right up to the tarmac. There were some random fires on the road. A burning tire. A pile of smoldering rags.

And jogging down the center of the road, a group of ten armed men in double file.

Mister Clean took one look at the small group of men in front of him and reacted immediately, whipping up his AK and depressing the trigger.

Modern combat is won in microseconds. It is broken down into tiny increments of movement that, each one, decide on life or death. A sword swings at a speed of approximately sixty feet per second and has a reach of three feet or so. A modern rifle round travels at two thousand feet per second and has a reach of over one mile.

It takes, perhaps, one eighteenth of a second to pull a trigger.

Mister Clean was quick. Very quick.

But Pete was The Prophet. A legend of war created by the one of the most ruthless armies on the African continent, if not the world. And he pulled the trigger one eighteenth of a second before Mister Clean.

Pete hit Mister Clean with a full one second burst from his CR-21. Ten high velocity rounds that simply tore the Xhosa leader in half. Perhaps a second and a half later Pete's three men opened fire. Short controlled burst of three or five rounds. Aimed.

One burst hit a case of Molotov Cocktails that Mister Clean's men were carrying, smashing them and igniting them at the same time. The mixture of burning oil and gas exploded in a massive fireball. Burning men ran screaming into the side of the wooden shacks which caught alight in turn.

Some of Mister Clean's men returned fire. AKs on full automatic. Hundreds of rounds tearing into the surroundings.

The collateral damage was huge. Innocent squatters ran from burning dwellings. Some already on fire. Others were cut down by the fusillade of indiscriminate automatic fire.

And at the other end of the street, crouched a girl in combat-chique makeup and a cameraman, filming the entire episode.

CHAPTER TWENTY-EIGHT

Bartholomew sat in the only chair in the hotel room and listened to Misty throwing up in the bathroom. It was a non-smoking room but, quite frankly, he didn't give a shit so he pulled out his pack of cigarettes and lit up. His hands shook. But he was alright. In the background he could hear Misty brushing her teeth. Rinsing. Splashing water on her face.

He went to the minibar, took out the entire compliment of little bottles of alcohol and threw them onto the bed.

'Misty,' he called.

'What?'

'When you finished up-chucking do you want a drink?'

'Yes.'

'What?'

'Anything.'

Bart chuckled. 'That's what I thought.'

He grabbed two glasses and then distributed the liquor fairly between the two of them. Misty got a blend of Cognac, vodka and rum. He got Gin, whisky and tequila. He threw some ice in.

'Here,' he held out the one glass to Misty as she came out of the bathroom. She took a sip.

'Jesus, what the hell is this?'

'Does it matter?'

She shook her head. 'No.'

He lit a cigarette for her and she accepted it gratefully. Drawing hard. Using the nicotine to calm herself.

'We're going to need more booze,' she said.

Bart nodded his agreement. Picked up the telephone, dialed room service and ordered a bottle of Jack Daniels.

While they were waiting for the drink to arrive, Bart pulled the television out of the cabinet and connected his camera to it. He rolled the tape back.

There was a knock at the door. Room service. He cracked it open. Accepted the bottle. Signed and handed over a tip in cash.

He filled their glasses, lit up another brace of cancer sticks and they sat together on the edge of the bed and watched the tape.

Then they re-wound it and watched again.

'Jesus Christ,' said Bart in an awed voice. 'Those guys were white.'

Misty nodded. 'But they were disguised as black men.'

Bart shook his head. 'There is something really fucked up going on here. We have got to get this feed to head office pronto. I think we got ourselves a story.'

***

Fat Man stood in the doorway to the hostel and looked out across the night-cloaked township. A pillar of flame lit up the smoky sky. An orange glow, like the aftereffects of an attack from some mythical creature.

'So,' he said to Garrett. 'You say it's the same guys that you heard this afternoon?'

'Garrett nodded. 'Same weapons. Same structure. Same combat skills. One group of undisciplined dudes with AKs and another group, highly trained, with 5.56mm weapons.'

'Who are they?'

Garrett shrugged. 'I don't know. Cops?'

'No,' denied Fat Man. 'Cops still use the R1 assault rifle. 7.62mmm. Very different sound.'

'Army?' suggested Garrett.

The Fat Man shuddered. Mounds of adipose tissue wobbled in sympathy. 'I hope not. The last time that the army came into Alex was in the early nineties. The government sent in 32 battalion. Scariest mother fuckers I ever laid eyes on. I tell you. When they were here you could leave a bag of money on the streets and no one would touch it. But they came with their own set of problems. Bad for business, you know. Hard to make a buck when the devil's sitting in your passenger seat. Petrus, what do you think?'

'Can only be the army. I'd like to know who the hell they're killing.'

'Well then,' said Fat Man. 'Go and see, why don't you.'

Petrus nodded. 'You coming?' he asked Garrett.

'Sure.'

'Leave the rifle,' said Petrus. 'Bring your steel. We go in quiet and stay quiet. Come on.'

Garrett handed his CR-21 to Fat Man and followed Petrus out into the smoke.

'We'll break left,' said Petrus. 'Go around the outside of the township and then cut in later. Come in from the side and see what we find.'

The two of them ghosted through the shacks. Garrett was amazed at how lifeless the place appeared. He knew for a fact that it was rammed full of people but he saw very few. They were huddled in their shacks, or seated in the shadows. Every person hidden away in his or her own private hell. Hoping that the violence would pass them by. Hoping that the flames wouldn't consume their meager belongings. Hoping that they could continue to live their insufficient, inadequate lives for one more day.

A dog ran out at Garrett, but before it started to bark it changed its mind and scuttled back into the darkness. Beaten before it had even begun.

The smoke covered all like a shroud.

A sixth sense raised the hair on the back of Garrett's neck. He trusted those senses implicitly. They had kept him alive for many years while all around him many others had died. He grabbed Petrus' shoulder and whispered urgently.

'Down.'

They dropped to the ground and rolled into the shadows.

A group of ten men walking two abreast loomed out of the smog.

Petrus waited until they had passed and then he lent close to Garrett. 'Xhosas,' he said. 'They are heading to the hostel.'

'What do you want to do?' Asked Garrett.

'There's only ten of them,' answered the Zulu.

Garrett nodded and pulled his machete from its holster.

Petrus drew his assegai.

They blended into the night. For this was what they did. They were the nameless fear in the dark. They were the feelings of dread that emanated from the shadows.

And as they moved on silent feet the Beast inside Garrett howled in exultation.

They struck.

The almost imperceptible whisper of steel through air.

The almost silent patter of blood dropping on dust.

The thud of two corpses falling to the ground.

The column turned around. Lying on the dirt were two of their comrades. Throats slit wide. Pools of blood. There was no one else to be seen. It was as if the very smoke itself had solidified, killed them and then once again sublimated into mere wisps of white.

The leader of the group, a veteran of the struggle called Elvis, called all of the men to him.

'Did anyone see anything?'

There was a general denial.

Elvis picked out three of them and pointed at the nearest shack. 'You three, go in there. Ask the people what they know.' He gestured to another three. 'The hut next to that one. Ask. We shall wait.'

The first three pushed open the door to the shack. It was too small for all three so only two went in. There was a family. Father, mother, three children. A brief conversation and they walked out. They looked at Elvis and shook their heads. Nobody had heard or seen any-thing.

The next three had the same results.

Not sure what else to do, Elvis got his men to strip the bodies of weapons, ammunition and valuables and they proceeded on their way. Eyes looking every-where. Bunched up. Now more of a gaggle than a column of warriors.

Something scuttled across the road in front of them. Elvis opened fire. A short burst from his AK. There was a whimper and a dog fell to the ground, its back legs reduced to tatters of flesh. It lay in the shadows and stared up at Elvis, its eyes full of disbelief. Man's best friend.

Elvis pulled a knife from his belt and handed it to the man next to him.

'Joshua, take this. Put the dog out of its misery.'

Joshua walked over to the mortally wounded canine. Bent down. There was a flash of light. A suggestion of movement in the dark.

Joshua's head fell from his torso. Severed cleanly with one cut. Blood sprayed high into the night. Deep red. A fountain of life.

After a stunned second of silence all of Elvis' men opened up at once, firing until their weapons were empty. But there was no one to shoot at. All they succeeded in doing was putting the crippled dog out of its pain.

Now the men were all huddled together. There was no logical explanation for what had just happened. It must be the *Tokoloshe*, a demon, hunting them.

Once again, they edged slowly down the street. All thought of their mission gone from their minds. Now, only survival.

Garrett and Petrus watched them from the shadows.

Then they followed.

CHAPTER TWENTY-NINE

Mason Parker was an old-fashioned newsman. He had started in the dailies and worked his way into television over a period of twenty-five years.

And he didn't abide people that considered the news to be simply an alternative form of entertainment. Another type of reality television. He believed that news should be hard-hitting, truthful and up to date. He also believed that anyone who changed their God given name to something as dire as Misty Malone would never be able to produce the sort of news that he considered to be, "the right stuff."

But Mason Parker was also old fashioned enough to admit when he was wrong. And boy was he wrong.

Before Bartholomew had downloaded the material and emailed it to head office, Misty had dropped in a voice over and then he had patched in a couple of talking heads close ups of her explaining where they were and exactly what was going on. The close ups were shot in amongst the pot plants in the hotel parking lot, but they were shot tight enough to disguise this fact.

Misty looked spectacular. Brave and sexy and serious. An action girl for the thinking man. And the action footage was like something out of a Rambo movie. Machine guns and hand grenades and firebombs.

Bartholomew had cleverly edited the rush with clips of colonel Zuzani denying that anything was happening and grainy shots of an armed man escorting Misty forcibly to her car. It was brilliant.

Within two hours it was being shown on every major network from CNN to BBC.

CHAPTER THIRTY

Two more of his men were dead. One moment they were shuffling along with the rest of the group and the next moment they were bleeding out on the road.

Truly, thought Elvis, we are being killed by spirits. He could hear one of his men's teeth chattering together in terror. It was one thing to die in battle but another thing entirely to have your life taken away by an evil spirit. Your ancestors would never accept you into the afterlife. You would be bereft, wandering the nether-lands for all eternity. Alone in the valley of shades.

The remaining five men were no longer heading in any specific direction. They were simply moving in the vain hope that movement would provide protection.

And then the smoke parted and the darkness came alive.

There was the whistle and flute of steel cleaving through the air. The wet thud of razor-sharp metal severing flesh and bone and sinew.

Two of the men managed to spray a few rounds into the air before they were cut down. Elvis stood frozen in terror as his men died all around him.

One of the demons coalesced into the figure of a man. A black man. He smiled.

Struck.

Elvis died.

***

Colonel Zuzani was worried. He had expected that, by now, someone would have brought him the Zulu, Petrus Dlamini. After all, the reward offered was spectacularly high.

Instead, however, it seemed as though Alexandra was fast becoming a war zone. If it escalated any more then he might be forced to send some of his men in. And that was something that he did not want to do. The losses would be unacceptably high.

He called sergeant Fumba over.

'Sergeant. Select five good men. I want them in plain clothes and well-armed. Send them into the township to do a bit of reconnaissance. I need to know what the fuck is going on in there.'

'I'll lead them myself,' said Fumba.

Zuzani shook his head. 'No. I need you here. Put corporal Ganda in charge.'

Fumba trotted off to do as told.

Within minutes the five-man squad was ready. They were dressed in their own home clothes. Non-descript jeans, cheap shirts and trainers. They each carried an R1 assault rifle. The South African made copy of the Belgian FN. A heavy, reliable weapon that packed a 7.62mm round.

At Fumba's instruction they walked off into the smoke and shadows, quickly disappearing into the bowels of the township.

Zuzani lit a cigar and lounged against the side of the armored car. He did not bother to speculate on what was happening in the township. He did not have enough information to do so. He would wait for the intel and then decide how to react.

Sergeant Fumba walked up and offered Zuzani a mug of coffee. He accepted with a nod. It was good. Hot, sweet and strong. It reminded him that he hadn't eaten since the morning and hunger struck him like a physical blow.

'Sergeant,' he said. 'Send one of the men to get me something to eat. Make it quick.'

Zuzani didn't have to wait long. One of the enlisted men brought over a take away carton of walkie-talkies, peri-peri gravy and pap. The dish got its name from the ingredients. Stewed chicken heads and feet – hence; walkie and talkie. The stiff boiled maize meal was used to soak up the fiery peri-peri. All in all, a good, traditional, lip-smacking meal.

Zuzani finished the food and wiped his hands on the seat of his pants. Just then his cell phone rang.

It was Manhattan Dengana.

'What the fuck are you doing?' Manhattan screamed down the phone.

'Calm down, Dengana,' retorted Zuzani.

'Calm down yourself, you moron. Have you seen the news?'

'No,' replied Zuzani. 'How could I have? I'm sitting next to an armored car outside Alexandra trying to sort out your fuck ups.'

'Well, you should take a look, because you're on it.'

'What channel?' asked Zuzani.

'All of them,' replied Dengana. 'And I mean all. Local, African, CNN, NBC, BBC. You're a world-famous fucking idiot.'

'Hold on, Dengana. What do you mean?'

'What do I mean? There's a third world war going on right next to you and all that you can do is deny that it's happening on international television. Listen to me, Zuzani, find Petrus Dlamini and find him fast. Do this for me and I promise you that I shall make you a wealthy man.'

Zuzani snorted. 'I am already a wealthy man.'

'I'm not talking BMW wealthy, Zuzani,' replied Dengana. 'I'm talking Lear jet wealthy. Now find that fucking Zulu and bring him to me.'

Manhattan broke the connection and sat back in his chair. His world was going to shit in a handbag and he was relying on a corrupt colonel and a right-wing nutcase to put it right for him.

He was less than confident.

But there was one thing that he could sort out with very little difficulty. He picked up the phone and dialed a private line at Doberman Security.

'Sampson,' he said. 'It's Manhattan here. How would you like to make a large pile of money? Good, I want you to send some men down to the Holiday Inn Plaza. There is a lady staying there, goes by the name of Misty Malone. She's a reporter. Find her and bring her to me. Thank you, my friend. See you soon.'

Manhattan hung up. He knew that what he was doing was not strictly expedient to his plans but sometimes you simply had to do something because you were pissed off with someone and wanted a bit of payback.

He smiled and lit himself a cigarette.

***

Bartholomew stood at the window and looked out at the car park. He breathed out and let his thoughts drift around like the cigarette smoke that he was exhaling.

It had been a good evening. The report had been a massive success and it looked as though there may even be awards in the offing. Misty was over the moon and the two of them had made a good dent in the bottle of Jack. Although it was late, neither of them wanted to sleep and so he had ordered room service. Steak, eggs, fries. A bottle of red.

Misty had taken a shower and was dressing in the bathroom while he stood and mused.

He hadn't always been a cameraman. In fact, he had been conscripted into the South African army in the mid 1980s and had signed on for long service, spending another five years in the force.

He had never risen above the rank of sergeant nor had he ever wanted to. During his combined seven years of service, he had fought in Angola, South West Africa, Mozambique and even Zambia.

He had been a good soldier. Not a great soldier. But the mere fact that he was still alive after seven years at the sharp end was proof of his quality. And the service had left its mark on him. The thousand-yard stare. The ability to react quickly and efficiently to aggression. And a sixth sense. A small danger-receptor in the back of his brain that had kept him alive during those incredibly violent years. A guardian angel.

It was this sense that started to buzz when he saw a SUV pull into the car park and four armed men dressed in black combat uniforms get out.

'Misty,' he called.

She walked out of the bathroom. Dressed in jeans, a green casual shirt and cowboy boots. Her hair was pulled back into a ponytail and she had the barest minimum of makeup on.

'What's up?'

'Listen, I think that we're in trouble.'

'Why?'

'Some men just arrived downstairs. Armed and in a rush. I don't know why but I just have a bad feeling. I think that we should get out of here ASAP.'

Misty looked as though she was about to argue but then she could see that Bart was being deadly serious.

'Okay,' she said as she grabbed her handbag. 'Bring your camera. Let's go.'

They left the room at a run, pulling the door closed behind them. They took the stairs instead of the elevator, leaving via the fire exit and into the car park.

As they got close to Bart's car someone shouted at them to stop.

'Sod that,' said Bart. 'Keep going.'

The man shouted again. His voice aggressive. Commanding.

They kept walking.

The night air was rent by the sound of a rifle shot. The bullet ricocheted off the concrete next to Bart's feet.

Misty squealed.

'Run,' shouted Bart. They sprinted the last few yards to the car. Bart pulled out his car keys and fumbled at the remote. The central locking opened and they both jumped in. Bart throwing his camera onto the back seat. There was another shot. This one took out the back passenger window.

Bart started the car, jammed it into gear and put his foot flat. With a screaming of tires and a plume of burning rubber the car leapt over the flowerbeds and straight into the road.

'Who the hell are they?' shouted Misty.

'No idea,' replied Bart. 'Cops maybe. Looked more like private security. Whatever, we are in some serious shit.'

'Can we go to the police?'

Bart shook his head. 'No ways. Those guys came in heavy. The cops must already know about this. The first cops that we see will run us straight in. It's my fault. I should have known that this would happen. We should have sent the report and then fucked off to somewhere safe. A hotel under a false name. Something.'

'What are we going to do?'

Bart kept his foot down. Driving fast. 'Don't know. Let me think.'

There was the sound of a siren behind them. A police car approached at speed. Bart rammed his foot down even harder, urging a couple more MPH out of the old tired engine.

One of the policemen lent out of the passenger window and started firing at them.

'Not good,' said Bart through clenched teeth. He dragged the car around a tight bend, barely sticking to the road. A bullet went through the driver side window.

'Great,' said Bart. 'A matching pair.'

'Do something,' shouted Misty unnecessarily.

The next shot smashed the back windscreen and lodged in the passenger seat.

'I've got it,' said Bart.

'What?'

'Where is the only place that the cops aren't going tonight?'

'No time for riddles, Bart. What are you going to do?'

'Alex,' he shouted. 'I'm going to Alexandra.'

'No way,' argued Misty. 'We'll get killed.'

'We'll get killed out here as well. Trust me. It's the only thing that we can do.'

Bart drove over the Sandton Bridge, cut right.

'But all of the roads are blocked by the police,' said Misty.

'I'm not going to take a road,' answered Bart.

He pulled into Arkwright Avenue, pulled hard left and then right and simply smashed through a wall and into a shack. The car steamed and spluttered to a halt. The two of them clambered out.

Two adults and a child sat staring at them. Around them the detritus of their tiny lives, smashed by the car. Misty opened her bag and pulled out a wad of cash.

More than six months' salary to the occupants, if they had been gainfully employed.

'Sorry,' she said as she threw the money at them. 'Got to rush. Bye.'

The police car screeched to a halt. Stood still. Red and blue lights flashing. After a while it reversed and drove off.

Bart and Misty headed back into the middle of the township.

CHAPTER THIRTY-ONE

Precious Ntuli was three years old. She lived in a dirt floor shack with two adults and three other children aged from four to seven. The adults were her mother and a man. It was not always the same man.

Unlike a standard western household there was no set bedtime. Nor set meal times. In fact, more often than not, there were no meals at all.

Precious did not know what time it was. She knew that it was dark hence it was nighttime. She knew it was late because everyone else in the shack was asleep.

She picked her way through the sleeping bodies, made her way out of the front opening into the alleyway, squatted down and urinated. After she had finished, she stood up and walked a few more yards, stopping to survey the night.

Suddenly she froze. Out of the shadows came four men. They carried assault rifles. Their faces were black but they were not black men.

The leader walked up to her. Loomed over her. Silent. Terrifying.

Precious whimpered in fear.

The man held a finger to his lips. Then he put his hand in his shirt pocket, and pulled out a candy bar. He gave it to Precious, rubbed her head and melted back into the night.

The little girl scuttled back to her dwelling and squeezed in next to her mother. Eventually she fell asleep, but for the rest of her life she would remember the night that the Devil gave her a candy bar.

***

Corporal Ganda and his four men sat in the dark on a street corner. Ganda had no intention of wandering around the township at night. He had decided to go in, find a secluded spot, wait for a couple of hours and then go back and tell Fumba that there was nothing to report. His men heartily agreed with this plan.

It was a good plan, as far as survival goes. It only had two major flaws and, to be fair, neither of them was actually corporal Ganda's fault.

Firstly, the corner that he had decided to wait on was a mere twenty yards away from Precious Ntuli's house and, secondly, there was absolutely no chance that Pete would be giving him a bar of candy.

The Prophet appeared out of the smoke five yards from Ganda and his men. He saw their weapons and reacted instantly. His first double tap took out the man on Ganda's right. The next slew the man on his left.

There was no thought in Ganda's mind of retaliation. He simply dropped his rifle and ran. A volley of shots followed, killing the rest of his men and leaving the corporal alone.

Running.

Running harder than he had ever run in his life.

Eventually he came to a main road. In the distance he could see the Casspir armored vehicle. Lights. More policemen. He staggered onwards, finally coming to a halt a few yards from the roadblock.

Sergeant Fumba ran forward.

Corporal, what happened?'

Ganda sank to his knees in exhaustion. 'We were attacked. They killed the men. An ambush.'

'How many?' quizzed Fumba.

Ganda shook his head. 'Not sure. Many. Maybe thirty. Maybe forty. We were totally outnumbered.'

'Were they Zulus?'

Ganda shook his head and took a breath. 'No, they were not Zulus. They were white men.'

Fumba did a double take, and then went to tell the colonel the news.

Zuzani thought for a while. Then he said.

'Impossible. He's lying. Bring him here.'

Fumba called Ganda over. The corporal had recovered enough to stand to attention and snap out a salute.

'Where is your rifle?' asked the colonel

'Lost it, sir. After I ran for my life.'

'How many assailants did you say?'

'At least forty, sir. Maybe more. We were ambushed. They must have known that we were coming. I fought bravely but to no avail.'

'And you maintain that they were white men?'

'Yes, sir,' Ganda nodded vigorously. Like a child affirming a story.

'Weapons?'

'Looked like CR-21s, sir.'

'Uniforms?'

Ganda hesitated. He knew that the men that attacked him were in civilian clothes. But he also knew that his story would appear more life threatening if they had been in uniform.

'Full combat gear, sir. Urban camo. Webbing, grenades.'

Zuzani pinched the bridge of his nose as he thought. What the fuck was going down in his city? Who could this third force comprise of?

'All right, Ganda. You did well. Go. Get some rest.'

The corporal saluted and left. Almost dizzy with relief that his story had been accepted.

'What do you think, Fumba?' asked Zuzani.

'I don't know. Americans?'

'Don't be stupid. Why?'

Fumba shrugged. 'Aliens? Time travelers?'

'So, you think that he's lying?'

Fumba gave the question serious consideration. After all, it was a life-ending question for the corporal. He shook his head.

'No. He was telling the truth. Exaggerating, maybe. But essentially the truth.'

'I need to make some calls,' said Zuzani as he walked towards his BMW. 'Go and tell Ganda to keep this to himself.'

***

Power Pulani was the man that Mister Clean had put in charge of the third group that was sent out earlier to attack the Zulu hostel. Power did not know that his was the last surviving group to have made it across the township.

He and his ten men crouched in the shadows behind a row of shacks next to the West side of the hostel. He looked at his watch. The other groups should be in position by now. Five more minutes and it would be time to launch the attack. Timing was important because, with all three groups attacking at the same time, the firepower from the hostel would be split. Diffused.

The second hand counted down.

Power stood up.

'Let's go,' he shouted.

The man next to him lit a Molotov and threw it. The firebomb fell short, exploding harmlessly on the concrete apron that surrounded the building.

The two other groups did not charge on account of all being dead.

As a result, every gun in the hostel was turned onto the single group of eleven men. The overwhelming quantity of firepower cut them to shreds before they had covered eight yards.

Two minutes later someone walked out of the front door with a fire extinguisher. They calmly put out the pool of burning petrol and went back inside.

Convinced that this was some sort of strategic distraction, Fat Man ordered his people to stay vigilant.

CHAPTER THIRTY-TWO

Bart and Misty sat huddled in a gap between two shacks. Misty was reading a leaflet using a tiny key ring led flashlight.

'Look,' she said to Bart. Thrusting the piece of paper at him. 'This is what that helicopter was dropping this morning. There's hundreds of them scattered around here.'

Bart read the reward notice through. 'It doesn't make sense,' he said. 'Who is Petrus Dlamini?'

'I am,' said Petrus.

Bart dropped the paper in shock and Misty squeaked like a trodden-on hamster.

Standing in front of them were two men. A black man holding an assegai and a white man holding a machete. Both of the weapons were dull with dried blood.

'Don't be afraid,' said the white man as he squatted down in front of them. 'My name is Garrett.' He held out his hand. Bart shook it first and then Misty. His hand felt strange. Like warm stone. Hard but somehow tactile. Misty didn't want to let go. It made her feel safe.

'We've been following you since you gate-crashed the party. Wondered what the hell you were doing here.'

'It's a long story,' said Misty.

'Make it short,' countered Garrett.

'We're reporters. TV. This afternoon we interviewed a colonel Zuzani about what was going on in Alex regarding the helicopter, the leaflets and the road-blocks. He was in the process of denying that anything was happening and spinning a story about a training exercise when a huge explosion and a bunch of automatic gunfire came from the middle of the township. Long story short, he kicked us out. So, we came back early evening to snoop around. We hadn't been in the township for more than ten minutes when we got involved in a firefight between two groups. Got it all on film.'

'Tell him about the white guys,' interjected Bart.

'Oh yes,' said Misty. 'One of the groups in the fight were white guys. They had blackened faces but when we ran the tape, we could see that they were white.'

Petrus and Garrett glanced at each other. The Zulu raised an eyebrow.

'Anyhow,' continued Misty. 'We went back to our hotel, edited the tape. Made Zuzani look a bit of a fool, I tell you. Sent the footage to head office and everyone went mental. It's being shown on every major and minor network in the world. So, obviously this pissed someone off because next thing we're being chased by the men in black, shooting at us and trying to kill us. We figured that the only place where the cops wouldn't come to get us was here. So – here we are.'

Garrett glanced at his watch. 'Look, it's just past two in the morning. You had better come with us, there's no way that the two of you would make it until daybreak. This place is full of uglies. Come on,' he helped Misty up. 'Follow. Tread softly, stick to the shadows.'

Petrus and he set off at a brisk walk and the reporters followed. Both Misty and Bart attempted to emulate the way that Garrett and Petrus moved. They flitted from shadow to shadow, often seeming to disappear completely even though they were directly in front of them. And their feet made no sound. It was like they walked above the earth and not on it. But it was impossible to imitate them. The reporters sounded like a herd of buffalo in comparison.

Bart was more impressed than Misty, for he had worked with Special Forces operatives before, albeit on a peripheral basis. So, he had seen the best. Or so he had thought.

But these two were in a different class. He knew beyond doubt that the only reason that Misty and he could see them, was that they allowed it. If they had decided not to be seen then their disappearance would be instant and unexplainable. They would simply become part of the night. There but not there.

Bart shivered with awe, and gave a word of thanks to the powers that be that they were being friendly.

Suddenly Garrett stopped. He signaled for them to get down. The reporters dropped to the ground. Petrus went down on one knee, assegai held ready. Garrett took a step to the right and simply vanished.

Twenty seconds later he appeared again.

'False alarm. Keep moving.'

'Jesus,' whispered Bart to Misty. 'My heart's going like a fucked clock. How you doing?'

'Scared.'

'Hang in there. We'll be alright.'

After twelve more minutes they turned another interminable corner and were face to face with the hostel.

'Home sweet home,' said Petrus. 'Follow us, don't talk unless spoken to.'

As they approached the building Bart noticed that at least ten weapons were trained on them from the ground and second floor windows. A group of five men came out of the entrance and walked towards them. They were all dressed in full gangster-bling. One even had four watches on his left arm and two on his right. All Rolex's. All fake.

The watch wearer appeared to be the leader. He walked in front and assumed more swagger than the others.

'Hey,' he greeted Petrus. 'How is it hanging, my nigga?'

Petrus took a step forward and casually backhanded the speaker so hard that he literally did a back flip, landing heavily on the concrete apron.

Petrus stood over him and shook his head. 'Boy, to you I am mister Dlamini. Or sir. I am no one's nigga.' He turned to face the other lost boys; his assegai held in front of him. 'Take note. All of you.'

He walked inside followed by Garrett and the two reporters. They went down the corridor to Fat Man's rooms.

'What is this place?' whispered Misty to Bart.

'It's an old worker's hostel,' answered Petrus on Bart's behalf. 'In the days of apartheid, the white government forced the black man to live in so called homelands. Separate states. But all of the work was in the white areas so the government set up a system of migrant labor. Male workers were forced to live in single sex hostels like this and go home to see their families during the holidays. Like prisoners on parole.'

'That's terrible,' said Misty. 'But what is this place now?'

Petrus grinned. There was no humor in the expression. 'Now. It's a single sex hostel run by a gangster and no one goes home during the holidays because this *is* their home.'

Petrus greeted the guards at Fat Man's door. They opened it and the group filed into the rooms. As usual, he was sitting on his sofa eating. A mountain of meat pies was stacked in front of him. On the side, four bottles of the ubiquitous green pop. He was dunking each pie in a large bowl of ketchup and putting it in his mouth whole. Two chews. Gone. Repeat. He ate three more, licked his fingers and beckoned at Petrus.

'Come, sit down. All of you.' He pointed at the pies and pop. 'Help yourselves. So, Petrus, what's happening?'

'Some weird shit going down, Fat Man. These are two reporters; they're hiding from the cops. We ran into a group of eleven Xhosas coming this way. Garrett and I neutralized them. Heard at least three other fire fights while we were out there.'

'One of those firefights was here,' said Fat Man. 'Ten Xhosas ran at us out of the shacks. Chucked a Molotov. We killed them. Very strange. Sort of a suicide attack. Expected them to start shouting "Banzai" at any moment.'

'Was probably meant to coincide with an attack from the group we sorted. That would have made more sense.'

'And the other fights?' asked Fat Man.

'Same group as before. The guys with the 5.56mm weapons. Two separate attacks. There's some sort of third force out there. The reporters claim that it's a small group of white guys.'

'That doesn't make any sense,' said Fat Man.

I know,' said Garrett. 'But I've been hearing that a lot tonight. The fact is, they're out there. They're there for a reason, so, for someone it makes sense.'

'There's only one person that it would make sense to,' said Petrus.

'Who?' asked Garrett.

'The Prophet. He's here for me.'

Garrett thought for a while and then nodded. 'I reckon that you're right. He thinks that he can use you to get access to the arms cache.'

Misty put up her hand. A child in a classroom. 'Excuse me, who is the Prophet? What arms cache? Why is Petrus on the flyers?'

'The Prophet is bad dude,' said Petrus. 'Ex secret police from the old days. The arms cache doesn't exist and he wants me because he doesn't know that it doesn't exist and he thinks that I can get it for him.'

'So,' said Misty. 'Basically, it's a war for no real reason.'

'All wars are for no real reason,' quipped Garrett.

Fat Man rammed down another brace of meat pies and then started speaking before he had quite finished them.

'Not a very complete explanation. Especially regarding the Prophet. Calling him a bad dude is just a bit Ninja Turtle. He's a seriously psychotic, dedicated right wing super-soldier. He's been shot over twenty times and still lives. It is said that he is un-killable. It is said that he actually died once and came back to life, but he no longer has a soul so you can't kill him again.'

Petrus laughed. 'You sound scared of him, Fat Man,' he teased.

'Damn right,' agreed Fat Man. 'Fucking terrified. Look, Petrus, I don't want to be "that guy" but you are going to have to do something about this. I can't afford to have the Prophet wandering around my patch with a bunch of armed apostles. It's a serious health risk and not good for business.'

'Don't worry about it, Fat Man. Garrett and I will go out now and find him. Sort this thing out.' He checked his watch. 'We got a few hours of dark left. Let's go. Fat Man, can you take care of these two?'

Fat Man nodded.

'Aren't you going to take any weapons?' Asked Misty.

Garrett pointed his machete at Petrus's assegai.

'I mean rifles and stuff.'

Garrett merely shook his head and he and Petrus departed, closing the door as they did.

Fat Man chuckled. 'Those are two seriously dangerous men.'

'More dangerous than the Prophet?' asked Misty.

Fat Man stared at her for a while before he answered. His eyes large and lugubrious. An old bulldog.

He shook his head. 'No. I was being serious when I spoke about the Prophet. He cannot be killed. I love and respect Petrus, but he and his friend will not be coming back. You cannot go up against the Prophet and live.'

'What will happen then?'

'Nothing,' answered Fat Man. 'The Prophet will have killed Garrett, and either taken Petrus hostage or killed him too and then he will leave. We will not be harmed. After that, the police will find out, and they will leave as well. Stay here a few days and then I will get some people to smuggle you out.'

'Thank you. Mister Fat Man,' said Misty.

He chuckled. 'Just, Fat Man, my dear. No mister.'

He shoveled in another meat pie.

CHAPTER THIRTY-THREE

Colonel Zuzani had to make a decision.

He turned to sergeant Fumba. 'Hey, Fumba. How much does a Lear jet cost?'

'Not sure. Boss. Eight, maybe ten million dollars, second hand. Why?'

'I want one,' answered Zuzani. He was quiet for a while as he thought. He had phoned around, dug deep into his contacts and pulled a few favors. But no one knew who the detachment of white soldiers was or what they were doing in Alexandra.

There was only one way that he was going to be able to sort this mess out and get the Zulu to Dengana.

He was going to have to take his men into the township in force.

'Sergeant, get our boys here. All of them. No outsiders. Get the outsiders to keep manning all of the roadblocks. Then issue our men with one hundred rounds of ammunition and two extra magazines for their R1s. Make sure that the machine gun in the Casspir has got at least one thousand rounds. We are going in at first light. We need to take the hostel in order to get Petrus Dlamini out.'

Fumba nodded and trotted off to get the men together. Within minutes people were running everywhere. Loading spare magazines, checking the machine gun, pulling on body armor.

And, a few yards away, hidden behind a wall, two of Fat Man's lost boys watched for a while. Then they stood up and sprinted back to the hostel, bursting through the front doors and running down the corridor to Fat Man's rooms. The guards let them straight in.

They both stood, panting. Neither spoke. Even though their information was red hot, to speak before Fat Man would be disrespectful.

Fat Man waited until their breathing had calmed down.

'Speak to me, boys. What's happening?'

Sipho took the lead. 'The cops are coming, Fat Man. They're tooling up for an assault. Big time, about fifty of them.'

Fat Man cursed. Every time Petrus Dlamini was involved in something it seemed to escalate into a full-blooded war of some sort. He was a man that thrived on battle. If Petrus was put into a cell by himself then, surely, thought The Fat Man, one of his hands would declare war on the other.

'What road will they be coming down?' Fat Man asked Sipho.

'They are in Arkwright at the moment. I think they will come down First Avenue.'

Fat Man pictured the layout of the township. The roads, alleyways, passages. The cul-de-sacs, dead ends. Lanes that looped back on themselves. A veritable maze. He imagined himself as a commander with fifty troops entering this maze. What would he do?

He wouldn't want to split his forces too much. That would leave them exposed. But he wouldn't want to attack only on one front. That would allow the enemy to concentrate their fire.

'They will come down First Avenue and Third Avenue,' he said. 'The bulk of the force will come down First. Do they have armor?' Sipho nodded. 'The armor will come down First Avenue. The secondary force will go down Third Avenue and then cut left. The armored column will attack from the West side and the secondary column will attack our front. They'll hit us hard and then stop to give us an opportunity to hand over Petrus to them. You two, get the lost boys here, quick. Move it.'

The two of them ran from the room, eager to do Fat Man's bidding.

Three doors down from Fat Man's rooms, Bart and Misty could hear the commotion outside. Running footsteps. Shouted commands. Urgency.

'Something's going on,' said Bart. He was sitting on a bed, back up against the wall. Misty was perched on the end of the same bed, her hands on her knees. The bed was the only piece of furniture in the room. And it smelled of old sweat and damp. There were no sheets, simply a faded gray blanket, cheap scratchy wool. Small areas of stiffness. Rank.

'I think we should go and see what,' said Misty. All too keen to get out of the fetid room.

Bart shook his head. 'No way, Misty. Fat Man told us to stay in this room until Garrett and Petrus got back and I for one am going to listen to him.'

They sat together quietly and listened to the hubbub going on outside. Suddenly someone flung the door open. Both of the reporters jumped in surprise. It was one of the lost boys.

'Come. Fat Man wants to see you.'

They followed him down the corridor to the rooms.

For once there wasn't food on Fat Man's table. This time it was covered with weapons. Two AKs, two Colt 45 pistols and loads of ammunition. Fat Man was thumbing rounds into spare magazines. Every now and then one of the shiny brass cartridges would drop from his hand, hit the table and roll to the floor as his massive fingers proved less than nimble for the task.

'Sit,' he commanded. They sat.

'I want you to stay in my rooms from now on. Tomorrow morning, around first light, elements of the South Africa Police Force are going to attack this hostel. We shall attempt to repel them. As representatives of the international press, I want you to know that we have done nothing illegal to deserve this. This attack is being perpetrated by corrupt members of the Police Force for their own personal gain. If we can win this, I would appreciate it if you could let the world know.' He held up one of the AKs. 'Can you use this?' He asked Bart. The cameraman nodded. The Fat Man threw the weapon at him and Bart caught it. 'And you,' The Fat Man asked Misty. 'Can you use this?' He held up one of the Colt pistols.

Misty nodded. 'My dad's from Texas.'

The Fat Man handed the pistol to her. 'You might need them, after all, the cops are trying to kill you as well.'

The behemoth stood up, put another 45 in his trouser pocket, grabbed the extra AK and then packed the spare magazines into his remaining pockets.

'Sipho,' he shouted. The door opened and one of the lost boys came in.

'Fat Man?'

'Call the rest of the lost boys in.'

Sipho went to the door and called. The young men trooped in. The lost boys. Hollywood wannabees. Rapper clones. But everyone a killer. Not for them the New York apartment and Versace suits. Instead, fake Rolex's, gold plated jewelry, well-used firearms and an early death.

Fat Man walked amongst them. Physically pushing them into three groups of three and keeping Sipho to one side. Then he pointed.

'Group one, group two, group three. Okay?'

They all nodded.

'Group one; I want you to clear everyone from First and Third Avenue. Tell them to leave if they value their lives. We don't want innocents to get harmed. Go, now.' Group one left. 'Okay, group two. Take five of the men and build a barricade across Second Avenue on the East side. I don't want any surprises coming from there. Chuck a few tires onto the barricade and light them. That should keep anyone out. Move it.' Group two ran off. 'Group three; take twenty men, fully armed, heaviest weapons that you can organize. Build another barricade across Third Avenue, just as it turns. When they come around the corner hit them with everything that you have and then retreat back to the hostel. Got it?'

The three lost boys nodded and headed off.

'What about putting a barricade across First Avenue?' Asked Bart.

Fat Man shook his head. 'No point. The Casspir would just drive straight through it. Waste of time.' He opened the door. 'Remember. Stay in this room.'

Bart stared at the AK in his hands. 'I hate these things.'

'What?' Asked Misty. 'Guns?'

'No. AK47s. They're evil. You know that the AK is responsible for more deaths than both of the atomic bombs put together? Hate them.'

He lit himself a cigarette and waited. Tense. Fearful.

CHAPTER THIRTY-FOUR

Petrus and Garrett slipped through the township. They were heading to a set of crossroads that they reckoned the Prophet would have to pass through in order to get to the hostel. They figured that, if he was after Petrus then that would be where he was heading.

As they moved Garrett's mind was spinning in overdrive. It would be wrong to say that he was scared of the Prophet. But he had spent time in his company. He had looked into his eyes. They were less than human. But they contained belief. Loads of it. He was a man who fought for a purpose. Contrary to what Fat Man had said, Pete was not a psychopath. He was a rational, thinking man, who had somehow, during his life, been broken beyond repair. A broken man.

He was human so he could be killed. But Garrett didn't want to kill him. For no other reason than he was sick of killing. He had come to South Africa to help his friend recover a kidnapped nephew and he had ended up killing over a dozen people. So far. On the whole these people were not his enemies. Most had done little or no harm to him.

And he had killed them. And, in doing so he had lost control of the Beast in him. Once again, he was becoming *Popobawa*. The demon. A man who lived to kill as opposed to a man that kills to live. It sickened him.

They arrived at the crossroads and paused. Blending in with the shadows. They waited. Silent. Still.

They didn't have to wait long until they saw something. A slight disturbance of the smoke. A subtle change in the quality of the darkness. Someone was coming.

Garrett waited until he saw the first man ghost into view. Then he stood up. Totally exposing himself to the enemy.

Petrus hissed in shock.

'Don't shoot,' said Garrett. 'We need to talk.'

The man froze, rifle at his shoulder, ready.

And behind him Garrett heard the faint metallic sound of an automatic rifle selector switch being flicked from safe to fire. The hair on the back of his neck rose up. He glanced sideways at Petrus who shook his head very slightly.

'Don't shoot,' repeated Garrett, softly. 'There are things that need to be said.'

'Turn around slowly,' said Pete. 'Both of you.'

The two of them complied. The Prophet stood about three yards from them. Half his face invisible in shadow, the other lit faintly by the ambient light. Like half a head floating in the air. A nightmare.

'How did you get there?' asked Petrus.

Pete didn't answer. He simply stared at them. A slightly puzzled expression on his face. Like they were some obscure species of animal that he was seeing for the first time. Eventually he spoke.

'What needs to be said?' he asked.

'The truth,' answered Garrett. 'The simple truth.'

'There is no truth anymore,' said Pete. 'Only varying degrees of lies.'

'Perhaps,' agreed Garrett. 'But what I am about to say is as close to the truth as I can get. Firstly, you need to know, there is no arms cache. It doesn't exist. Never did. It was a propaganda exercise dreamed up by the Inkatha party to big themselves up before the elections. No cache. No secret weapons. Nothing. That is the truth.'

The Prophet's eyes bored into Garrett. The void in the darkness.

Then he nodded. 'You speak the truth.'

Pete let his rifle drop, the barrel facing the ground. He signaled to his men who appeared out of the darkness. Quizzical but silent.

'There's more,' said Garrett. 'You aren't the only one looking for Petrus. The cops dropped off leaflets this morning offering a reward for anyone who could bring him in alive. I'm surprised that you haven't come across one. They're all over the place. That's why the cops have bottled up the area. They don't want Petrus or me to get out.'

'That doesn't make sense,' said Pete.

Garrett chuckled and shook his head. 'Why does everyone keep saying that? Of course it makes sense. It simply doesn't make sense to us. What we need to do is figure out who it makes sense to and then ask them what the fuck is going on.'

As Garrett was talking the sun began to rise. All around him came the sounds of the township coming alive for the day. People started to drift out of their shacks. Fires were restocked and the acrid smoke pall started, once again, to thicken.

'Look,' said Petrus. He pointed in the direction of the hostel where one could see two massive pillars of black smoke boiling into the sky. 'It's tires,' he continued. 'Someone is burning a shit-house worth of tires. That can only mean one thing. Fat Man has set up barricades in the roads.'

'I think that we should go and check out what's happening,' said Garrett.

Pete stood still. His mind was in turmoil. Emotions boiled close to the surface but he did not show any. To do so would be weakness. But he needed to know what was going on. Why were the police looking for Petrus? Who else was involved? Was this the end of his dream of a white homeland?

He gestured to his men. 'Come. We go as well.'

Garrett nodded his acceptance but Petrus looked less than happy. His hatred of the Prophet ran deep, the result of many years of apartheid atrocities compounded by his recent aggression against Petrus' own family.

However, Garrett reckoned that it was better to have The Prophet where you could see him. As opposed to wondering where he was. What he was doing.

The six of them set off at a trot. All around them the township dwellers continued their lives. Some glanced at the group of armed men as they jogged by, others ignored them. Some children pointed. Some mothers hid in their huts. Simply another day in one of the most violent places in the world.

CHAPTER THIRTY-FIVE

Manhattan rose early, as was his custom. He had slept in the room attached to his office and managed to grab two or three hours of restless slumber.

By now he had resigned himself to the fact that his plan had not worked. The margin call that he had gambled on would come due in the next couple of hours when the stock exchange opened in Johannesburg. He would lose, not only his entire life but also the life's savings of all of his partners. They were small men but they were spiteful. They would gang together and seek retribution. They would want him dead. But they would have to catch him first.

He had a number of passports under a variety of names and nationalities. They were not fake in that they were all the genuine article, save the personal information on each one.

He had not chosen the clichéd destinations either, preferring the more European countries as opposed to South America, Mexico or any African states. Instead, he had a French passport, a Canadian, a Spanish and a British one. He had some contingency funds. Not enough to last more than a couple of months, but he was a resilient man. Bright, well-educated and ruthless. Like a phoenix from the ashes, he would rise again.

He decided to take a long shower. Shaved and dressed in one of his tailored English suits. Turnbull and Asser shirt, Izingara tie.

Then he phoned a local restaurant and ordered a breakfast to be delivered. Steak, eggs, hash browns, freshly squeezed orange. He did not order coffee as he had a superb bean-to-cup espresso machine in his office and fancied himself as a bit of a barista.

While he waited, he turned on CNN. It was the usual crap. Natural disaster in India. Some or other African shithole declaring war on some other unknown African shithole. Muslims blowing up stuff. Americans telling them not to.

And then the video of colonel Zuzani making a fool of himself. Christ, thought Manhattan, apparently the same video had gone viral on You Tube overnight. Three hours after it had been shown on TV some bright spark had put it to music and it already had twenty million views.

Someone knocked on the door and Manhattan went to open it. It was the deliveryman with the breakfast. He carried it in and laid it on the table in the corner of the office. Manhattan signed the bill and added a tip. He had an account so there was no need for cash to change hands.

In the background the newsreader said something that tapped at Manhattan's consciousness but he ignored it. He pulled the cling film off the breakfast plates and the mouth-watering smell of steak wafted up.

Then it hit him. He frantically grabbed his remote control and activated his cable hard drive, rewound the news and listened again.

And the video footage that the world is now referring to as "Zuzani's Farce" has shown the South African government up in a less than favorable light. So much so that when the markets opened this morning the Rand was trading over twenty percent down on yesterday's price.

Manhattan rewound again…

…when the markets opened this morning, the Rand was trading over twenty percent down on yesterday's price.

Again…

…when the markets opened this morning, the Rand was trading over twenty percent down on yesterday's price.

Twenty percent.

Manhattan Dengana had just made a paper profit of over Five Hundred Million Dollars.

His hands shook as he switched off the television.

Five hundred million dollars. Not as much as he had hoped to realize with his original plan but it was still a very large sum of money. Particularly if he didn't share it.

And why should he? He was the one who had made the plan. He had taken the risks, used his influence to change the market. It was him. All him. Fuck them all, he said to himself. It's mine.

He opened his briefcase to take another look at his passports and decide which one to use.

***

Zuzani rode in the passenger seat in the Casspir. Surrounded by two-inch steel plate and bullet proof windows. In the cupola behind him rode sergeant Fumba, in control of the 7.62mm FN Machine gun.

Thirty of his men trotted behind and next to the armored vehicle. He had sent the other twenty men to attack via Third Avenue in order to hit the hostel on two fronts at once. As they moved forward, he saw two massive pillars of black smoke rise into the air. One seemed to be coming from opposite the hostel and the other from the corner of Third Avenue.

The radio in the cab crackled into life. At the same time the rip and pop of automatic gunfire could be heard coming from Third Avenue.

On the radio was Corporal Twesi. 'Colonel, we are under attack. There are roadblocks and barricades of burning tires. Please advise. Over.'

Zuzani thumbed the return button. 'No advice needed, Twesi. Just fight your way through. Out.'

A sound like hail striking tin rang out and Zuzani saw two of his men drop to the floor. Flowers of red blooming on their body armor as the assault rounds punched through it.

Behind him the 7.62 mm hammered back. Spraying ten rounds a second back at the attackers. The policemen also opened up with their R1s. But Zuzani couldn't see whom they were shooting at as the attackers had already vanished into the maze of shacks.

The Casspir ground forward. Another brace of men dropped as the snipers on the top of the hostel started picking them off. Fumba swept the machine gun back and forth along the roofline, hosing the area with full metal jacket slugs.

The detachment in Third Avenue was not doing as well. They had no armored support and no squad support weapon. Corporal Twesi had ordered them to go to ground and return fire. But they were horribly exposed to the men behind the barricade. A Molotov cocktail flickered over the barricade and exploded amongst the police. One of them caught alight and rolled around on the ground screaming as he burned to death.

More Molotovs followed.

'Get back,' shouted Twesi. 'Back, back. Move.' He wanted his men out of range of the petrol bombs. They retreated in good order, laying down as much covering fire as they could. They pulled back to the corner and regrouped.

'We need to flank them,' he said to his men. He pointed out four of them. 'You four stay here and keep returning fire. The rest of us will split into two groups and go around the barricade. We go straight through the shacks into the back alleyway, get behind them and hit them from there.'

The remaining four started to return fire while the two groups made their way into the back alleys.

Corporal Twesi had done well. He had retreated in good order. He had rallied his men and he had come up with a good plan. Strictly speaking it wasn't his fault that the plan was blindingly obvious. As both teams broke through into the parallel alleyways, they found themselves ambushed by a group of heavily armed Zulus with shotguns and AKs.

They didn't even have time to fire back before they were all dead.

Then the ambushers came pouring out of the surrounding shacks and obliterated the team of four that had stayed behind.

Sipho called for order and gathered everyone together. As a group they started to run back to the hostel to support Fat Man.

***

Garrett, Petrus and Pete had watched the skirmish with interest.

'They did well,' said Petrus.

Garrett shrugged. 'Not much of a contest.'

'The real problem is the other attack,' added Pete. 'Armor, machine gun. Proper leadership. That's where this will be decided.'

'Come on,' said Garrett. 'Let's go take a look. See what we can do.'

***

Bart and Misty sat crouched against the wall under the small windows. The room was covered in shards of glass from the windowpanes that had been blown out in the first few seconds of gunfire.

Misty was shaking with a surfeit of adrenaline and fear.

Bart looked bored.

'How can you be so calm?' she asked.

'I'm not.'

'But you look…I don't know…bored.'

'I am. I hate sitting and doing nothing.'

'But aren't you scared?'

Bart chuckled. 'Absolutely, totally fucking terrified. Who wouldn't be?' He lit a cigarette. Misty could see a slight tremor in his hands as he did. But it was well controlled.

Another burst of machine gun fire strafed the building. Two rounds found their way through the windows and ricocheted around the room, shattering a lava lamp in a shower of blue and red dye.

Bart stood up and fired back, not aiming. Simply random return fire.

'Why did you do that?' shouted Misty.

'Makes me feel better.'

Misty popped up, stuck her 45 out of the window and pulled off a few shots. Then she dropped back down, a huge grin on her face. 'Hey, you're right. I do feel better.' She sprang up again and fired until the magazine was empty. 'Take that, you mother fuckers,' she yelled before she went to ground again.

Bart laughed out loud. 'Fuck me, Rambo.'

She took the cigarette from his hand, took a drag and then started giggling like a schoolgirl. Within seconds the two of them were lying on the floor, such was the strength of their tension relieving laughter.

Bart sat up. 'Take that, mother fuckers, 'he laughed.

Misty was attacked by a further fit of giggles.

Another long burst of machine gun fire raked the building. One of the copper jacketed rounds buzzed through the window, ricocheted off the back wall and hit Bart in his left eye, tearing through his brain and exiting through the back of his skull.

Misty screamed.

And screamed.

***

Fat Man's troops were being beaten. There was no other word for it. Superior training and firepower were getting the best of them.

Garrett, Petrus and Pete watched from two streets away, on the top of a rundown wooden house.

'They need to stop the armored vehicle,' said Garrett.

'They can't, replied Pete. 'It's impervious to small arms fire and grenades. As long as the cops just keep inching forward, fire and movement, they'll take the hostel.'

'What about Molotovs?'

'*Ja*,' said Pete. 'That would work, but you won't get close enough. The 7.62 will cut you down.'

Petrus had been staring for a while, not contributing. Eventually he spoke. 'Hey, I know that monkey on the machine gun. Also, the fucker inside the Casspir. It's sergeant Fumba and colonel Zuzani. That's Zuzani's private army.'

'What, not real cops?' asked Garrett.

'No, they are real. It's just that they answer only to Zuzani. He's probably the most corrupt cop in the South African Police Force. And that's saying something.'

'So why is Zuzani putting so much on the line to get hold of you?' Asked Garrett.

'I'll tell you what he's not doing it for,' replied Petrus. 'He's not doing it for the shitty little reward. He doesn't need the money. That can only mean that he's working for someone else who is either very high up or who has offered him a shit-house full of cash. Or both.'

'Is there anyone that he usually works for?'

Petrus nodded. 'Word is that he does a lot of wet work for Manhattan Dengana. Although that's strictly rumor.'

'I would like to have a talk with this Zuzani character,' said Pete.

Petrus snorted. 'No problem. Let's just wander down there and ask him if he wants a chat.'

The Prophet's eyes bored into Petrus. 'I didn't say that it would be easy. I merely said that I would like it to do it.'

Petrus bristled. 'Okay, what do you suggest, mister fucking know everything?'

Pete took a step towards Petrus who brought his assegai up in front of him. Old hatreds crackled between the two warriors. Palpable in their intensity.

'Settle,' said Garrett. 'Not the time and place. So, what do you suggest, Pete?'

'First,' said Pete. 'I think that we should get into the hostel.'

'I agree,' said Garrett. 'Let's get closer, wait for a lull in the fighting and then gap it. Petrus, you take point. They'll recognize you, so hopefully they won't shoot us.'

'Oh, don't worry,' replied Petrus. 'They won't shoot me.' He looked at Pete. 'You though, I'm not so sure about.'

The group climbed down from the roof of the shed and started towards the hostel. They got to the end of the street and then waited. After a few minutes there was a lull in the firing and they all sprinted. One of the lost boys pushed the lobby doors open for them and they piled in.

Fat Man stood against the one wall. AK in one hand and 45 in the other. His chest was covered in blood. Two of the lost boys lay on the floor, their jackets covering their dead faces. Three others stood next to Fat Man, handguns in hand.

'Hey, Petrus,' he said. 'Good to see you. Who's the company?'

'This is…' Petrus hesitated. 'Pete. These are his men.'

'Hello, Pete. So, what brings a bunch of armed white folk into my township?'

'Long story,' grunted Pete. 'There's stuff that I need to find out. You know that you're getting your ass kicked out there?'

Fat Man nodded. 'So it would seem. Never fought against a Casspir with a machine gun before. Evil bastards, aren't they? Hey, Garrett, those reporters that you brought in. Sorry man, the one's dead. The guy took one to the head. I've had them cover the body but the girl's gone mental. I've had to give her a fucking wheelbarrow full of ammo for the AK. She's been shooting at everything that moves out there. Maybe you should go and have a talk to her.'

'Will do, Fat Man. Then I'll come back. We need to talk tactics. See how we can win this thing.'

The Fat Man gave a thumbs up. 'I like the way you think.'

Garrett walked down the corridor and opened the door to Fat Man's rooms. Misty was reloading magazines with FMJ ammunition. Thumbing them in frantically. Talking to herself as she did so. The words were formless. More cadence than actual speech. A child humming to keep the monsters away.

'Misty.'

She looked up and smiled. An expression as brittle as Edinburgh crystal. 'Hi there,' she said. 'Just reloading. Do you want to help?'

Garrett sat down next to her. He didn't touch anything.

'I think that I've killed at least three of them,' Misty said. 'Good, huh?'

Garrett put his hand over hers. 'That is good, Misty. Maybe you should take a break now. A short rest.'

'No ways,' she shook her head empathically. Whipping it from side to side. She finished reloading the final magazine. But Garrett picked up the AK and held on to it.

'Give me my gun,' yelled Misty.

Garrett shook his head.

She swung at him and connected hard, her ring splitting open the flesh on his cheek. Blood ran down. Garrett didn't flinch. He simply sat. Holding the AK. She hit him again. And again.

Then she fell against him, weeping. 'He's dead. I told him to come here and he's dead. I killed him.'

'No,' said Garrett. 'None of this is your fault. This is Africa. People die. You're alive. Mourn his death and remember him, but be happy about your own life. Appreciate how precious it is.'

Misty's sobs slowly hiccupped to a stop and then she drew a deep breath.

'I'm sorry,' she said.

'Nothing to be sorry about,' replied Garrett. 'This will soon be over. Not long. I want you to wait here, Misty. Your part in this is finished. It's not your war.'

Misty looked at Garrett. 'Is it your war?'

Garrett shook his head. 'No. It's never my war.'

'Then why are you fighting it?'

Garrett stood up. 'Because I don't know how not to,' he replied. He grabbed his and Petrus' CR-21 assault rifles from the corner of the room where they had left them, pocketed the extra magazines and left the room, closing the door behind him.

When he got back to the lobby Fat Man had his shirt off and one of the lost boys was bandaging his chest. A round had struck him high on the left side, passed through the flesh and exited under his shoulder. The lost boy had packed the wound with some sort of powder and was wrapping a bandage around his massive chest.

'How is she,' he asked.

'She'll be fine,' replied Garrett. 'Tougher than she looks. Listen, Fat Man. Have you guys got any drums of gasoline? Big ones.'

'Sure. We run the electricity in this place from a gas generator. Got drums of the stuff out back.'

'Great. Get the boys to bring a drum here. Also, forty pounds of sugar or whatever amount they can find, some duct tape and a pump.'

'A pump?'

'Yeah, you know. For pumping tires up. A foot pump.'

Fat Man nodded at the three lost boys. 'You heard the man. Go to it.'

They scampered off. Killer puppy dogs.

Outside the battle was hotting up again. The machine gun firing in short bursts, targeting the windows. The return fire was sporadic as the hostel dwellers ducked for cover. After a few minutes the three lost boys came back. Two were rolling a forty-gallon drum of fuel and the third was carrying a sack of sugar, a roll of silver duct tape and a foot pump.

Garrett stood the drum upright, pulled out a knife and punched a small hole in the cap. Then he unscrewed the cap and poured the sugar into the petrol. After that he put the cap back on and squeezed the hose from the foot pump into the hole. Then he sealed it tight with duct tape.

'Do you have any tracer rounds?' He asked Fat Man who nodded and told one of the lost boys to fetch a carton of them from his rooms.

Garrett started to pump vigorously, pushing hard until he could pump no more. Then he bent the hose over, twisted it and wrapped it with duct tape to seal it airtight.

Now he had a forty-gallon drum mix of gasoline and sugar under huge pressure, or to put it another way, a homemade pressurized napalm canister.

Pete raised an eyebrow. He was impressed. Garrett had just cobbled together a weapon of mass destruction out of a handful of household ingredients. And he had come up with the plan on the fly, showing an intellect higher than most that Pete had come across before.

The lost boy returned with the tracer rounds and handed them to Garrett, his expression respectful.

'I need an AK,' said Garrett.

Fat Man handed over his. Garrett ejected the magazine and thumbed out the first five rounds, replacing them with the incendiary tracer rounds.

'Now what?' asked Petrus.

'Now we wait,' answered Garrett.

'For what?'

'For the cops to make their offer. Won't be long now and they're going to tell us to give them Petrus or else.'

'What will we do then?' asked Fat Man.

'Well, we shall give them Petrus, of course,' said Garrett with a grin.

'Thanks, my friend,' countered Petrus. 'I always knew that I could count on you to watch my back.'

'Seriously now,' said Garrett. 'We need to get this drum as close to the Casspir as possible. I figured that the best way would be to simply roll it down the road into them. There's enough of an incline. And I reckon that the best way to do that would be to bring Petrus out on the right side of the building to hold their attention while a few of the lads roll the drum down the road. As soon as it gets close enough, I shoot it with these tracer rounds, the drum ruptures and the pressurized, thickened gasoline squirts out all over the Casspir.'

'What if they shoot Petrus?' asked Fat Man.

'No,' Garrett shook his head. 'They want him alive. He'll be fine. I think.'

As Garrett was talking the firing outside hiccupped to a stop. Then they heard the feedback from a megaphone.

'This is colonel Zuzani of the South African Police Force. I have a warrant for the arrest of Petrus Dlamini. Please note that there is also a substantial reward being offered for the same. I recommend that you bring Dlamini to us or we shall press on with our attack and this time we will not hold back. I will give you five minutes to think this over.'

Garrett looked at his watch. 'In four minutes send Petrus outside with two of the lost boys flanking him. Both with rifles. Let's make this look like we're forcing him to go. Stick close to the building and walk towards the right side. We will push the drum out. They'll see us for sure but I'm banking on them not registering what's going on.'

There was a general murmuring of agreement.

'Pete, 'said Garrett. 'If this works then Zuzani is going to come piling out of the Casspir at speed. We need to be there to welcome him so that we can drag him back here to chat. Can your boys cover us?'

Pete nodded. 'My boys will cover us. I'll be there with you.'

'So, are you with me?'

Pete nodded again and then smiled, he liked this foreign warrior. Bright, courageous, quick and deadly. His kind of person. The fleeting smile changed his face entirely, like a different person had taken his place. Then it dropped and the Prophet returned. Dedicated, black-eyed and fanatical.

The seconds and minutes ticked by. Slicing off little increments of life as they marched by. One. Two. Three. Four minutes.

'Right, gentlemen,' said Garrett. 'Let's do it.'

Petrus walked out of the front doors. Behind marched the two lost boys, AKs trained on him. The one lost boy jabbed Petrus with the barrel of his AK, getting into the role of aggressor.

'Hey,' whispered Petrus. 'If that goes off and shoots me, I swear that I'll fucking kill you. So cut it out.'

The lost boy stopped.

Garrett waited until Petrus was half way to the waiting Casspir.

'Let's go,' he said. Pete and his three soldiers ran out first, keeping low and scuttling to cover. Then Fat Man, a lost boy and Garrett pushed the drum out. After two or three yards, Garrett stopped helping, as it was unnecessary. Fat Man's prodigious strength was more than enough to power the drum along at speed. Fat Man twisted the drum so that it faced directly down First Avenue and started rolling it faster and faster.

Petrus saw it coming and shouted out to attract the policemen's attention.

'Hey, Zuzani you useless piece of crap. Still got your pet monkey with you, I see.'

Sergeant Fumba stood up out of the machine gun cupola. 'Say what you want, Dlamini, but your so called friends have sold you out. So, who's the monkey now?'

The drum of napalm trundled down the road and thumped up against the front wheels of the armored car.

Fumba looked down. 'What the fuck is that?'

'Hey, monkey boy,' shouted Petrus. 'Duck.'

Garrett opened fire.

All five tracer rounds struck the pressurized drum. It ruptured and ignited at the same time, spewing gallons of viciously burning fuel all over the Casspir and the surrounding troops. The effect was even more spectacular than Garrett had hoped for. The entire front of the armored car lifted six feet off the ground and then thumped back, bursting the burning front tires as it did so.

Garrett and Pete immediately sprinted towards the burning armored car. Pete's soldiers covered them, squeezing off well-aimed double taps at the enemy to keep their heads down.

As predicted, Zuzani kicked open his door and jumped from the stricken armored vehicle. Pete ran through the flames and smashed him on the jaw with the butt of his rifle. Garrett caught him before he hit the ground, flung him over his shoulder, turned and ran back to the hostel.

By the time he and Pete bundled back into the lobby Petrus was already there.

'Now that,' said Petrus, 'was good fun.'

Garrett stared at the Zulu prince for a full three seconds. 'You know, my friend, sometimes I wonder about your sense of fun.' He shook his head.

Petrus grinned even wider. 'Happy days, my man. Happy days.'

The two friends laughed out loud, venting the adrenaline. The fear. Reveling in the mere simplicity of being alive.

CHAPTER THIRTY-SIX

Manhattan Dengana, now known as Patrick Delanus, accepted a welcome cocktail from the first-class stewardess. His choice of where to go had been simple. He merely chose the first available first-class flight out of Africa.

Before he left, he had consolidated his massive winnings and transferred them all via a maze of unlinked accounts to a final one in the Isle of Manx. It would be virtually impossible for anyone to trace where either he, or the money had gone.

He had packed light. There was no need for anything. He would be able to buy everything that he needed when he arrived. The only thing that he had brought, aside from a change of underwear, socks and a laptop was his Baobab medal, Supreme Councilor class with its cream and gold ribbon. He was inordinately proud of the large, rough rectangle of gold with its graphic of the Baobab tree in the middle. For exceptional service in industry and economy. He grinned to himself, and for the personal enrichment of Manhattan, no Patrick Delanus.

He took a sip of the cocktail It was good. Some sort of fruit and vodka mix. Perhaps a touch of Cointreau.

Delicious.

***

Zuzani's forces had been routed. The hulk of the Casspir listed to one side. A ship wrecked in a sea of flame. Bodies lay scattered around the hostel. Fat Man had sent men and women out to care for the wounded from both sides.

Now Fat Man, Petrus, Garrett, Pete and Misty were in Fat Man's rooms. Lying on the floor, hands zip tied behind his back, lay Zuzani. His head lolled from side to side as he rose through the darkness of his unconsciousness into the light.

Petrus threw a glass of green pop into his face and he spluttered awake and sat up. He glared at the people around him.

'What the fuck do you think that you are doing?' He asked. 'Do you have any idea who I am?'

'Why?' asked Garrett. 'Have you forgotten?'

Zuzani glared at him. 'Let me go this instant and I might let you live.'

Garrett shook his head. 'No can do, colonel. Someone wants to talk to you.'

'I won't tell you a thing,' said Zuzani.

'I don't care,' said Garrett. 'I'm not the one who wants to talk to you. He does,' he pointed at Pete who stepped forward and went down on one knee next to Zuzani.

The colonel took one look at Pete and jerked back, as he desperately tried to wriggle away.

The Prophet smiled, all teeth and no emotion. 'I see you know of me, colonel,' he said.

Zuzani nodded, his face slack with fear. 'You are the Prophet. Please don't kill me.'

Pete said nothing for a while. He simply stared; his dark eyes boring into Zuzani's soul. 'Why did you attempt to kidnap Petrus Dlamini?'

'It was for you,' said Zuzani. 'Manhattan Dengana told me to, so that you could get weapons to further your cause.'

Pete flinched as though he had been slapped. 'Why would Dengana want to further my cause. It was diametrically opposed to his.'

Zuzani shook his head. 'No. He was your benefactor. It was he who supplied you with the money. Isaac was only a go between. Dengana was speculating on the money markets. He needed the Rand to drop in value and he needed to put a specific time frame to it. So, he set you up to do something that would reflect badly on the country's stability and he could reap the rewards. Look, I'm not sure on all of the details, only what I picked up along the way. But the fact remains, *I* was helping *you*.'

Pete stood up and walked to the small window. Stood looking out, not seeing. His careful planning, the lives lost, his dream of a white homeland. All a farce conjured up by one of his bitterest enemies. Such was his shock that he was struggling to breath. Every intake of air, a careful guided thought as opposed to an autonomous function. He could feel his heart hammering in his chest and he wondered idly if he should bother to keep it beating. As if he had a choice.

He noticed a hawk flying high in the sky. Watched it as it used the thermals from the burning armored car to rise itself up. Higher and higher, until it was a mere speck in the silver blue of the heavens. A bird of war. Implacable. Relentless.

Suddenly he turned, walked back to Zuzani, dropped to one knee again, grabbed the colonel by the throat and, with casual strength, snapped his neck.

The Prophet let the limp body fall to the floor as he stood up and left the room. He walked down the corridor, called his men to him and strode from the building.

Nobody said anything for a while until Petrus spoke.

'Now that,' he said, 'is one seriously intense dude.'

Fumba sat in the leather wingback chair and stroked his cat. The side of the sergeant's face had been badly burned. There was no skin and the gleam of white bone stood out on his cheek. He had also been shot in the stomach and his right thigh.

The pain was beyond intense, but Fumba ignored it.

After the Casspir had been destroyed and Zuzani captured, Fumba was at a loss. Despite the fact that he was nominally second in charge of the colonel's operation he was, in actuality, mere muscle. He needed to be led. Without a leader he was a rudderless ship.

So, he had taken the BMW with his cat inside and driven to Manhattan Dengana's offices. Looking for someone who could tell him what to do. But when he got there the offices were empty. The lights were still on but the doors had been left unlocked. Abandoned.

The sergeant sat down behind Manhattan's desk and stroked his cat.

He heard the outside office door bang open and the sound of footsteps. Two people. The footsteps got closer. The office door was flung open. Two men walked in.

'Hey,' said Petrus. 'It's monkey boy. Where's Dengana?'

Fumba shrugged. 'Gone.'

'Where?' Asked Garrett.

'I don't know. I don't know anything.'

'Well then,' said Petrus. 'You're not much use to us, are you?'

Fumba shook his head. 'No. Are you going to kill me now?'

Petrus stared at the sergeant for a while. 'Is that your cat?'

'Yes.'

'What's its name?'

'It depends,' replied Fumba. 'It changes all the time. It used to be Heckler. Then Mbejane.'

'What is it now?'

'Cat.'

'Big points for imagination, monkey boy. Who'll take care of it if I kill you?'

'No one,' answered Fumba. 'It will take care of itself.'

Petrus shook his head. 'No ways. It's too young. Still a kitten really. I tell you what. When it's older and can take care of itself, maybe then I'll come and find you and kill you. Okay?'

Fumba nodded. 'Whatever, I don't care.'

'Come on,' said Petrus to Garrett. 'It's over. Let's blow this place and go home.'

The two men left.

Fumba sat for a while. He was thirsty but he couldn't move. He no longer had the strength to raise himself out of the chair. He knew that he was bleeding internally. On the plus side, the pain had gone. Instead, his whole body had gone numb. As if he was detached from it.

He tried to close his eyes so that he could rest.

But the lids would not work.

He really ought to decide on a permanent name for the cat, he thought. It was unseemly for a pet not to have a name.

His head flopped forward onto his chest, his breath hissed in and out. Shallow. Insufficient.

Dingaan, he thought. I'll call him Dingaan.

His breathing stopped.

The cat purred.

After a while it jumped down from his lap and walked away.

CHAPTER THIRTY-EIGHT

Sifiso had woken before dawn. He had crawled out of his blankets and gone outside to look at the cows in the central kraal. He did this every morning without fail. He loved the huge, doe-eyed bovines with their slow gentle ways and their cud chewing and their flatulence.

He would normally watch them alone for half an hour or so until the rest of the village was up and about. Then he would go back to his hut and eat a huge bowl of well-salted maize meal porridge. As much as he wanted.

This morning, however, he was not alone. A tall, well-built man had already been standing at the fence when he got there.

'Good morning, little big man,' greeted Petrus.

Sifiso laughed. 'Hello, but how can I be little and big at the same time? That's not right.'

'Well,' replied Petrus, 'you see, I look on the Big Man as having been your father, so, when you grow up you too shall be known as The Big Man. But until then you are still little. So; Little Big Man.'

Sifiso nodded, his expression serious. 'Yes. That is good. I will be Little Big Man.'

'So, Sifiso,' continued Petrus. 'You like the cows?'

Sifiso nodded.

'That is good. Cows are very important to us. They are our wealth. Are you happy here?'

Again, the little boy nodded. 'Very happy. I get porridge every morning and meat every night, and I am never scared when I sleep.'

Petrus rubbed him on the head. 'That is good. Now that you are more settled, I am going to get someone to organize your schooling. I want you to work hard every day and keep out of trouble. Okay?'

Sifiso nodded. 'I want to go to school. Then when I grow up, I want to be a doctor. Doctor Big Man. Then I can save people's lives and no one will ever have to die again.'

'That is a good ambition, Little Big man. Very good.'

Petrus lit a cigarette and wondered. He wondered how many people he had killed in order to save lives. And he wondered if it had been worth it.

Behind him he could hear the village awakening as the sun broke the horizon. The banging of pots and pans, the buzz of conversation, the crackle of the cooking fires. The mundane sounds of normal life.

As opposed to the hammer of automatic gunfire, and the screams of the wounded and the dying.

And he knew that, yes, it had been worth it. Because someone had to do it. Someone had to be that guy.

Because, in its purest form, the act of retribution provides symmetry, the rendering of payment for crimes against the innocent. But the danger lay in furthering the cycle of violence.

Still, thought Petrus, it was a risk that had to be met because the greater offense would be to allow the guilty to go unpunished.

And that he could not do.

Patrick Delanus, AKA Manhattan Dengana, took a reverential sip of the Lagavulan thirty-year-old Scotch, closing his eyes in pleasure.

He stood on the balcony of the Royal suite in Edinburgh's finest and oldest hotel. A world of marble and thick wool carpets and butlers and crystal. A world that was a million miles away from the stink of Africa.

He raised his glass to take another sip, but before he could it was knocked from his hand. It fell to the floor and smashed.

Something slipped over his neck. Pulled tight. Restricting his breathing.

He tried to fight back but his legs were kicked out from under him, driving him to his knees. He scrabbled frantically at the cord around his neck. Fingernails clawing at his own flesh. Tearing and cutting.

It takes a long time to throttle someone to death. Especially when you are using the cream and gold ribbon of the Baobab Medal, Supreme Councilor class, for exceptional service in industry and economy.

Eventually Manhattan Dengana's lifeless body slipped sideways onto the floor.

Garrett stood up, threw the medal onto Manhattan's chest, and left the room.

The guilty had been punished.

Retribution had been served.

****

I really hope that you enjoyed this book.

If you wanted to have a chat or give me some advice then please email at zuffs@sky.com. It is my personal email and I will get straight back to you.

If you would like to read more Garrett & Petrus adventures then please take a look at the next book: Here are a couple of chapters – take a look and see what you think…

THE BLOOD OF LIONS.

Thanks again

Craig

There was a festival atmosphere about the procession. Five Toyota pickup trucks each towing a converted horse trailer. The first four trailers each contained approximately two and a half tons of Southern White Rhinoceros. *Ceratotherium simum simum.* The largest living land mammal after the African Elephant. Five thousand pounds of pissed-off-Pachyderm reduced to the state of a docile pet dog by the introduction of 2 milligrams of Acepromazine, via a dart gun.

The fifth trailer had two occupants. The game rangers had already dubbed them Dick and Dom. A pair of male rhino calves. Overlarge three toed feet, massive upright ears and tiny little nubs of horn. They too were sedated and lay snuggled together, snoring and whistling in their sleep, their juvenile lips turned up into permanent half-smiles as they gamboled and capered in their dreams.

The rangers had round up the Rhinos that morning, tracking them through the night and darting them as soon as the sun had risen to provide enough light to shoot by.

And now they were on their way to the Kharma Rhino reserve in Botswana. It had been deemed of vital importance to move as many rhino to Kharma as possible. This was due to the fact that well over one thousand Rhino had been killed in South Africa the year before, whereas there had not been one death in the Kharma Rhino Reserve in the entire twenty four years since its inception.

Unfortunately, due to the vast amounts of red tape, combined with the lack of both funds and manpower, the parks trust had only managed to relocate a mere six rhino during the last twelve months. A failure to perform that bordered on the ridiculous.

Malusi was riding shotgun in the second pick up; his Remington pump action lay across his knees. Since his recent qualification from the South African Wildlife College and his being hired as a conservation officer by the Kruger National Game Park, this was the most exciting day that he had ever experienced.

He was convinced that the future of the country that he loved would come to rely more and more on the tourist industry and as far as he could see, the tourist industry in Africa would be dominated by tourists seeking the wild game experience.

That, combined with his genuine love of animals, is what had driven him to study and to pursue his current career.

The convoy drove slowly and carefully down the rutted dirt roads that led from the reserve. The morning sun blasted the land with a white-hot heat that robbed the scenery of all shadow, rendering the vista as a flat, two-dimensional photograph, printed in shades of browns and olive-greens and khakis.

The dust from the lead pick up hung in the dead air like a massive ochre storm cloud, coating all the followers in its fine, yellow-brown talc.

Malusi placed the butt of the Remington on the floor between his legs and pointed the barrel out of the window. Each pick up had a driver and a passenger that had been issued with a weapon. Malusi had his shotgun, and the remaining rangers carried the venerable R1 assault rifle. A weapon that had last seen service in the 1980's during the South African bush war.

They all handled their weapons with a certain amount of familiarity, but it was patently obvious that they were not professional soldiers. A few hours on the range does not a military man make. These were Game Rangers. People trained in conservation and animal husbandry. Weapons were there for defense against wild animals and even then, only as a very final resort.

But, as rhino poaching had become so endemic, the rangers had been forced to swap their 375 bolt action hunting rifles and shotguns for weapons more suited to warfare than to animal control.

Malusi glanced upwards, squinting through the dust-covered windscreen. High above them wheeled a White Backed Vulture, a magnificent bird with a wingspan of over seven feet. It had been following them since they had set off that morning.

The young Zulu shivered with superstitious dread. The vulture was never a good omen. Particularly one showing such persistence.

The land mine was a Chinese version of the type 72. Twelve pounds of high explosive jammed into a steel container. It was capable of damaging a main battle tank to the point of putting it out of service.

Its effect on the thin-skinned Toyota commercial vehicle was nothing short of catastrophic.

The blast severed the cab from the load area, tossing it up into the air in a storm of steel and flame. Both the driver and passenger were killed instantly as the shock wave smashed their brains, shattered their bones and crushed their internal organs. The trailer and rhino that they were pulling crashed into the back half of the vehicle and flipped over, landing on its side. Even though the rhino was sedated it screamed and bellowed in terror, thrashing its massive head from side to side, slashing its flesh open on the jagged exposed blades of metal sticking out of the sides of the damaged trailer.

The gigantic shock wave punched Malusi's driver in the chest, causing him to spasm at the wheel, jerking the pickup into a hard right hand skid. The trailer jackknifed behind them, tearing itself off the hitch and rolling into their vehicle.

Malusi kicked the door open, stepped outside and stood, swaying, next to the ruined cab. His mouth hung open as his brain tried desperately to catch up with the surrounding reality.

The other pick-ups came to a halt and men started to jump out and run towards him. He saw their mouths working and he knew that they were talking to him. Shouting even. But his ears were ringing and the huge amounts of sensory overload had caused auditory exclusion and tunnel vision.

He shook his head and, all of a sudden, sound and vision returned.

And then the air around them came alive with the spiteful crack and buzz of high velocity metal. Bright scars appeared in the door of the pick up and one of the other game rangers flew backwards as his body was riddled with shot, blood spraying from him in a viscous mist of bright red.

Someone shouted. 'Machine gun.'

Malusi grabbed his shotgun from the cab and looked for someone to shoot at but, before he could, his breath was driven from his body as three copper-jacketed steel rounds slammed into him, picking him up and throwing him over the hood of the vehicle.

Some of the rangers began to return fire but they were soon cut down by the overwhelming quantity of ordinance arrayed against them.

Malusi slid down off the hood and lay on the dry African earth. An ant crawled over his open eye. He tried to blink but he couldn't. He wondered if he was breathing. And if so, how? He could hear his heart beating. A drawn-out rushing sound. Like water being drawn from a hand-pump. Slow and laborious.

He could hear men talking. Laughing. He smelled cigarettes.

Then the sound of a petrol driven chain saw starting up. The ragged growl of machinery.

The horrific sound of the saw hacking through flesh and bone. The bellowing of the rhinos. A volley of shots.

'The horns,' whispered Malusi to himself. 'They're cutting out the horns.'

He tried to move.

He had to do something.

He had to stop this.

A shadow fell over him. Someone was standing there.

'Hey, check this out,' they said.

A strange accent. Russian? Polish?

'This fucker's still alive.'

'Kill him.'

'No,' whispered Malusi. 'Please.'

He felt a boot against his face. A push. Rolling him over onto his back. The barrel of a rifle. Held close to his eye. So close as to be out of focus.

You never hear the sound of the shot that kills you.

***

The vulture was patient.

It sat in the thorn tree and waited.

Eventually the men left and quiet settled once more over the African veld. It flapped its large wings as it dropped to the ground.

Spoiled for choice it simply waddled over to the nearest body and started to feed.

Malusi had been right - the bird had been a bad omen.

The worst.

Tai Zeng stood still and waited for his attackers to come to him. There were three of them. Large men. Each one topping his mere five foot five by more than six inches.

The first one struck out. A straight punch to Tai's head. A powerful blow that would knock the smaller man to ground. Once down it would be easy to dispatch him with either a stamping kick or a simple snap kick to his head.

But the punch never landed.

Tai moved inside the swing and, using the tips of his fingers, he delivered a Fut Sao blow to his opponent's underarm. Striking where the lymph nodes, arteries and veins conglomerated. The man stiffened and fell to the floor as his entire nervous system simply shut down. Tai casually kicked him in the side of the head as he stepped over him, making sure that he was completely out of the fight.

Again, Tai stood still, the only part of him moving were his eyes as they flicked between his two remaining opponents.

They both attacked at once, driving in from opposite sides, hoping to confuse the master.

But it was to no avail. Tai launched a counter attack, smashing his open hand into the one man's Brachial Plexus on the side of his neck. Cutting off his blood supply and incapacitating him with a single blow.

Then he swivelled and, using the Ving Tsun Kung Fu method of rolling punches, he drove the final opponent backwards, throwing five punches in under a second. It was like being hit by a machine gun and the man was unconscious before his limp body even reached the floor.

Tai Zeng stared down at the three unconscious victims, his face a mask of scorn. The three men had been personally recommended by the local dojo as sparring partners worthy of respect. They were far from it. Rank amateurs.

Tai had studied Ving Tsun under the auspices of the late master Ip Man. It was an explosive fighting style that combined close quarter combat with solid defensive techniques and rapid counter strikes. It had been popularised during the late seventies by the film star Bruce Lee and many westerners referred to it as Wing Chun Kung Fu or often simply, Kung Fu.

Typically the western mind had, once again, misunderstood the entire concept. Kung Fu referred to any skill that takes time to master. Only westerners thought of Kung Fu as unique to the martial arts.

Tai grabbed a small hand towel and left the dojo, wiping the sweat from his face as he did so. He closed the door behind him and walked to his desk, throwing the towel to the floor.

Pressing the button to his intercom he buzzed his secretary.

'Mingyu. Come through.'

While he waited, he stood at the floor to ceiling window and gazed at the view. One hundred stories below him, Victoria Harbor stretched from left to right, crowded with all manner of boats from ancient Junks to modern Sunseekers. It was a vibrant mélange of both color and culture.

The skyline was dominated by the massive brooding hulk of Mount Austin, or The Peak as it was known locally.

But the view had little to do with why Tai leased the ultra-expensive office space on the 100th floor of the International Commerce Centre in Kowloon. He was there for other reasons. It was the tallest building in Hong Kong and it shared its address with prestigious firms like Morgan Stanley and Credit Suisse. Highly respected international companies that Tai Zeng felt himself to be on a par with.

Also the floors 102 - 118 were leased by the 5 star Hong Kong Ritz Carlton hotel in which Tai leased a permanent three bedroom suite at a cost of five thousand dollars a night. Although that was his permanent residence, he also had a one hundred- and twenty-foot

Sunseeker yacht berthed at The Royal Hong Kong Yacht Club, one of the city's most exclusive clubs. Yet another accoutrement that he had acquired more because he thought that it was the correct thing to do, rather than any love for the water, or for seagoing dwellings.

Mingyu entered through the main office door and closed it behind her. Barely topping four feet in height, she was like a person in miniature. A neat boyish figure and short black bob. She wore no makeup save for a thick line of kohl around her large brown eyes. Her lightweight cotton dress reached just below her knees, loose fitting and plain. No jewellery.

'Mingyu. I need you to book me a flight to Vietnam. Next week. Two day stay. Same hotel as always. Also, set up a meeting with the Police Commissioner as soon as. Mutual ground. Perhaps one of the restaurants in the hotel. I need to speak to colonel Chang sometime this afternoon, check out the time difference between here and Zimbabwe and place the call around four o'clock our time.'

Tai droned on, dictating a long list of tasks for his tiny assistant. She took no notes but simply nodded at the end of each command to show that she had taken it in.

While Tai talked, he slowly stripped off. Peeling his sweat-wet training clothes from his body until he was completely naked. Then he grabbed the diminutive Mingyu, bent her over the desk and pulled her dress up around her waist. She wore no underwear. He entered her roughly, grunting with the effort as he continued to dictate his seemingly endless list of tasks.

Mingyu didn't react at all, save to keep nodding at the appropriate times.

When he was finished, he withdrew, wiped himself off with his discarded shirt and waved a dismissal to Mingyu.

She bowed once and left the room, her dark eyes expressionless. Her face a mask of blank submissiveness. All feelings buried deep by the large monthly check that she received combined with the knowledge that people did not resign from the employ of Tai Zeng. You worked for him until he retired you.

And one did not want to be retired by mister Zeng.

Tai crossed the office to his built-in closet and selected a traditional black silk Zhongshan Zhuang or Chinese Tunic Suit, as favoured by Chairman Mao. He slipped his feet into a pair of silk slippers and then poured himself a drink. Two fingers of the ubiquitous Johnnie Walker King George V that was so popular amongst the Hong Kong elite. No ice.

He sat at his desk and savoured the smoky taste. It hadn't been so long ago when his entire month's earnings didn't come close to being enough to afford a single bottle of the premium spirits. Growing up in Kwun Tong along with over half a million other dispossessed people, crammed into an area hardly capable of supporting even a tenth of that number.

He remembered well those first days in the gangs. Barely a teenager, he had been accepted as a Blue Lantern in the local Triads. An uninitiated member, lowest of the low. Called on to do all of the worst jobs. But he worked hard and soon became known as a youngster to rely on. An up-and-coming member who never refused a task no matter how dangerous or humiliating.

He had been promoted to the level of a 49'er before anyone else that had joined with him and as an initiated Triad member, was exposed to his first tastes of both power and privilege.

Within a few short years he achieved the rank of Enforcer, a rank on a par with a White Paper Fan administrator or a Straw Sandal liaison officer. It was at this stage that Tai decided to branch out on his own. The Triad system, unlike the Italian Cosa Nostra, is more than happy for its members to go their own way, as long as they retain a loose affiliation to the Triad structure and pay their dues every month.

Now Tai ran his own empire. Even though his rank in the Triads had never officially been raised, he was considered by all to be at least on a level with a Vanguard or Operations officer and perhaps even as high as the Deputy Mountain Master, who was second in charge.

Tai's main strength was his innate ability to plan for the future. He played the long game in a structure that so often looked for the quick profit. The big score. As such he had used his growing influence to inveigle his way into the new Red Chinese government structure that now controlled Hong Kong, sowing his seeds and laying his lines of influence and power in all aspects from customs and excise, to police and military envoys.

As a result, when China had started their big military push into Africa; Tai Zeng had been there, riding on the coat tails of the People's Army.

Now he owned, to all intents and purposes, his own crack military team whom he used to control his substantial interests in the region.

Officially the team were actually a part of the People's Army and were ostensibly under the control of Colonel Jin Chang.

Colonel Chang had been transferred to Zimbabwe along with his assistant, Master Sergeant Lu Feng and a detachment of thirty two Nanjing Flying Tiger special forces troops as a roving fast reaction squad to provide security and advice to the Zimbabwean army.

In reality colonel Chang and his detachment were simply another cog in the mechanism that made up Tai Zeng's criminal engine. And Tai ensured Chang's loyalty by paying him vast amounts of money and allowing him to pursue his own private business ventures as well.

Although Tai had his fingers in many pies including illicit diamond buying, drugs, ivory and prostitution, his main income was generated through the illegal poaching and distribution of Rhino horn.

He had teamed up with a Ukrainian gangster by the name of Viktor Hubenko and together, they were responsible for the deaths of around ten rhinos a week. At the going price of one hundred and twenty thousand dollars per horn, this equated to six million dollars a month, or seventy two million a year. This, combined with his other criminal pursuits grossed over one hundred million dollars per anum.

But the money was not that important to Tai. Even though he lived a relatively lavish lifestyle he found it hard, if not impossible, to spend more than ten million a year. The rest of his income was a mere set of numbers on a scorecard. A handicap level at golf, a social ranking.

A way to distance himself from the poor shoeless orphan brought up in the slums of Kwun Tong.

Garrett had been the game warden on the laird's estate for over five years now. He had known the laird for most of his life and he owed him more than he could ever repay. He had taken Garrett in when his parents had died, leaving him an orphan at the age of ten. The laird had sent Garrett to the same boarding school that his sons had attended and he had supported Garrett's decision to join the British army.

There had been a long period, a few years, when he had lost touch with the young soldier. It was during this time, when Garrett had had retired from the army and had pursued far more lucrative work as a private contactor or mercenary soldier, fighting mainly in Africa, a continent that was rife with constant conflict.

The lifestyle had not been good to Garrett, driving him deep into the black heart of war, stripping him to the bone and exposing his dark inner core. Unleashing a violence that ran fast and furious through his soul. Releasing a Beast that found itself capable of the most violent of deeds and actions.

Finally Garrett had escaped from Africa. Running from his own lack of humanity. Hiding from The Beast.

The laird had taken him in, given him a job as his gamekeeper. He had sensed that Garrett needed help but he had never questioned him. Never pushed him. He had simply allowed him free rein.

Garrett soon discovered that The Beast was an integral part of himself and you cannot run from yourself. So he locked it up in a cage and refused to feed it. And he lived alone. Not lonely but singularly, at one with the Highveld. The outdoors.

However, there were still times when The Beast crashed through the bars and came out into the light.

Bad times.

Garrett tried to avoid them.

But sometimes they were thrust upon him.

That morning his laird had come to him. His granddaughter had gone missing. She had been incommunicado for almost a month now. There was no huge panic on. It was suspected that she was with her boyfriend, a ne'er-do-well that she had met after she had dropped out of university. A small time drug dealer and even smaller time artist, some twelve years her senior.

Garrett had never met him but he knew Alicia well. A product of the most expensive private schools combined with almost unlimited access to wealth. Her parents would describe her, if they bothered, as willful, fiery and possessed of her own mind.

Garrett, on the other hand, would describe her as a stone cold, spoiled brat.

The laird doted on her and, in all fairness, he was the only human being that she treated with anything approaching respect.

Regardless, the laird had asked Garrett to track her down and there was no way that he would ever refuse him.

He had been provided with Alicia's cell number. He had tried it and it had gone straight through to messages. The only other info that he had was the last known address of her waster boyfriend, Rafe Hinds.

Now Garrett was currently heading for that current address, driving the estate Defender Land Rover. He had been on the road for over three hours, driving through the lashing rain, the skies as gray as the Atlantic Ocean, visibility less than fifty yards and the merest hint of sun, so weak as to necessitate the use of headlamps even during the day.

He was using a satellite navigation system and it informed him that he was nearing his destination. A road in the notorious East End area of Glasgow.

Garrett had never been there before but he did remember hearing that a man born in that deprived area had a life expectancy some nine years less than a man born in rural India.

The area itself was a depressing mélange of old and new and completely fucked up. Crumbling tenement blocks next to unfinished new builds and dilapidated Victorian houses. He drove past a building that looked derelict but, as he got closer, he saw a hand painted sign, lit up by a red spotlight. The sign said, "Adult Fun".

A monstrous doorman stood outside the rotting wooden front door, rain sluicing off his black mackintosh. Shining off his shaven head. Dripping unheeded from his broken nose. He stared as Garrett drove by. Eyes like two pebbles in a mountain of flesh. Gorilla in the mist.

Three hundred yards further on he reached his destination. A row of seedy Victorian houses. Red brick and broken sash windows. Tottering chimneys. Front doors scabbed by peeling paint. Drifts of refuse. Milk cartons, crisp packets, newspapers, used condoms. Needles.

Garrett felt his first niggles of worry. He had known that Alicia had fallen in with a less than salubrious bunch but he had always understood it to be an upper-class dalliance with the lower middle classes. Nothing too rough or untoward. A childish poke in the eye or middle finger to parents considered too cold or distant or remote.

A callow cry for attention.

But this area and the vista that presented itself to him at the moment smacked of something deeper. People who lived in places like this did not do so through choice or through rebellion. People who lived in a shithole like this did so because they had nowhere else to go.

They had no further to fall.

Garrett pulled up against the sidewalk, stepped out, locked the door behind him and headed to the second house along. Number 223.

The door, at one stage, had been red. Now it was a pale pink. A badly painted anarchy sign had been scrawled across it and, under that, a swastika.

The swastika had been painted incorrectly so that the arms went the wrong way.

A billboard to both ignorance and stupidity.

He thought about knocking but then decided against it and simply tried the door. It was open, the lock long since smashed and hanging free. He pushed it and walked in.

The building stank of damp and sweat and urine. And something else. Some sweet undefined stench. Heady yet, at the same time, nauseating. Garrett was not familiar with it.

He walked carefully through the ground floor, opening doors and peering into rooms. Three rooms downstairs, all uninhabited.

There was also a kitchen. An old ceramic sink, cracked, half full of an unidentifiable black oily substance. A few broken cupboards. An old refrigerator. The door open. Bizarrely, the internal fridge light still worked and it shone brightly from inside the white, glossy interior. A pathway to another world.

There was a bathroom. The bath had been removed. If it had been an old cast iron one then it had most probably been sold for scrap. There was also a toilet. Water ran from the top of the cistern, the flow mechanism long since broken and the plumbing continued to attempt to fill an already overfull tank. The toilet itself was blocked with an old T-shirt that had obviously been used when toilet paper had run out. Garrett grimaced at the smell and left the room, heading for the stairs.

He climbed the creaking staircase and started to search the next floor. The first room, like the ones below, was empty.

When he entered the next room, he almost didn't recognize her.

She sat crossed legged on the floor. Her long blonde hair had been hacked short and her eyes were sunken into their sockets. A lava lamp bubbled away in the corner, distorting the shadows and painting all in the hues of a nightmare. Blood red and frozen blue.

The floor was slick with vomit, the stench sweet and rotten at the same time. Garrett had seen this before. It was a fairly common side effect from injecting heroin. But to the user, the minor inconvenience of throwing up all over yourself was inconsequential compared to the resultant high.

There were two other people in the room. Both men. They sat together on a single bed, passing a joint between them.

'Who the fuck are you?' One asked.

Garrett ignored him completely.

'Alicia,' he said. His voice low. Non-threatening. 'Your grandfather is worried about you. He's been trying to call.'

The young girl stared at him for a while. 'Where's he?'

'He's at home,' answered Garrett. 'He asked me to find you. To take you home.'

She shook her head. 'Not going home.'

'I think that you should, Alicia. Just to show him that you're okay. You don't have to stay.'

Again, she shook her head. 'No. Stay here.'

'You heard her,' said one of the men from the bed. 'So fuck off now, why don't you?'

Once again Garrett merely ignored him. 'Come on, Alicia. You can't stay here. It's not good. Come back with me. Speak to the laird. No worries. Things will be alright.'

The man who had been talking to Garrett stood up off the bed, walked over and grabbed him by the shoulder.

'Look, mate. Fuck off before I make you fuck off.'

Garrett didn't bother to even look at the man. He simply backhanded him across his face. Blood sprayed from the man's smashed nose as the blow lifted him up and deposited him back on the bed. Unconscious.

Alicia screamed. The other man jumped off the bed and ran from the room.

'You hit Rafe,' shouted Alicia.

She jumped up and ran over to the prostrate man, patting ineffectually at his face in an attempt to revive him, tears welling from her eyes.

'He's hurt. You hurt him.'

She attacked Garrett, both hands swinging at him, pummeling him in the chest and shoulders.

Garrett stood and accepted the abuse. Eventually she ran out of energy and slumped down onto the bed.

'Sorry,' said Garrett. 'He'll be fine. Alicia, you need to come back with me.'

'Fuck you.'

Garrett shook his head. 'Afraid not, my girl. Now look, I don't want to get all demanding and asshole about the whole thing but the laird asked me to get you home, so there is no longer any choice in the matter. You are coming back with me. Accept it, embrace it, argue with your grandfather. I am simply the messenger.'

'You can't tell me what to do,' she hissed at him. 'You're just the hired help. A jumped-up gardener. Fuck you, you servant.'

Garrett nodded. 'That's correct. I am a servant. But I am not your servant, Alicia. I serve your grandfather. So, pack your shit, or don't, we are leaving.'

As Garrett finished speaking the bedroom door crashed open. The runner and four more men walked in. The runner had called in reinforcements. Garrett could see instantly that the four newcomers were a different breed. True bottom feeders. These were not artists experimenting with different levels of consciousness. Nor were they upper-class brats falling off the rails.

These were the real deal. Men who had grown up hard and gotten harder. Tempered through poverty and prison. Through gang wars and institutional violence. Urban hyenas.

And even lions are wary of hyenas.

Garrett stepped back, placing his back into a corner. Cutting down their field of attack.

'Who the fuck do you think you are?' Shouted one of the newcomers. Shaven headed, sleeve tattoos. Enough metal in his face to satiate an inner-city scrap merchant. 'You can't come in here and harass my peeps. You made yourself a big mistake.'

Garrett held up his hands. 'Look, mate. I'm sorry. Didn't mean to offend. I've simply come to pick up Alicia. We'll go, no more trouble. Okay?'

The man shook his head. 'No. Not okay. Firstly, you disrespect my peeps, you disrespect me and my boys. And if you disrespect me and my boys then we gotta teach you a lesson.'

As he spoke he drew a knife from his belt, flicking it open with a well-practiced movement. Behind him his boys also drew their knives.

'Listen, Aaron,' said Alicia. 'He's just a fucking moron. He works for my grandfather. Let him go. He won't come back.'

Aaron looked at Alicia and smiled. 'You're too soft hearted, babe,' he said. 'You don't understand the rules. He dissed us so he gotta pay.'

'Look,' said Garrett. 'There's no need for all of this. Tell you what, you guys back down, I take Alicia and that is that. No one loses.'

'No,' countered Aaron. 'I got a better idea. I cut you real bad, you learn a lesson. You lose.'

Garrett sighed. He had attempted to negotiate. He had done all that he could to offer the hyenas a soft option. But they had refused. Now, all that would happen is that they would work themselves up until they were angry enough to do something and then they would attack. Probably not all at once. In all likelihood, Aaron, who was obviously the leader, would strike first and then the others would barrel in straight afterwards.

Garrett decided to hurry the whole process on and simply stepped forward and punched Aaron.

A straight right, using the power of his hips and shoulders. Striking with the full weight of his hyper-toned, two hundred and twenty pounds of sinew and muscle. Driving a knotted fist of rock-hard calloused bone into Aaron's nose. Crushing it almost completely flat and rendering its owner immediately unconscious for the foreseeable future.

Garrett stepped back from Aaron's prostrate body. Pausing to, once again, give an out to the remaining hyenas. Another offer of the soft option.

It was a mistake.

The sound of a safety catch to a Browning Hi-Power 9mm semi-automatic pistol being released is infinitesimally small. Probably akin to a damp match being broken in half. Or a copper penny being dropped onto a carpet.

But to Garrett it was as loud as a shouted profanity in a church.

He had heard that exact, or similar, sound so many times in his life that it was as common as the sound of a friend's breath. A lover's cough. An undertaker's knock.

It was the sound of imminent death.

Without warning The Beast crashed through the bars of its prison. Howling and slobbering it ran free.

Free to hunt.

Free to fight.

Free to kill.

Garrett grabbed the pistol and yanked it hard sideways, snapping the gunman's finger with a sharp crack. Then he twisted the gun back and away from him with a savage punch, literally tearing the gunman's finger off.

The dismembered finger dropped to the floor and blood arced across the room as the man sank to his knees, squealing in shock and agony. Garrett kept hold of the weapon, grasping it by the barrel.

Then, using the pistol as a club he hammered it into the second man's temple, dropping him to the floor like a felled tree.

The third man received an elbow to the nose and then a savage blow to the top of his head as Garrett clubbed him into unconsciousness.

The runner, true to form, sprinted from the room and ran out into the street as self preservation wiped all thoughts of heroism from him in one sphincter-tightening moment.

Garrett flipped the pistol over, grabbing it by the butt. Then he stood over the gunman, the barrel pointed unwaveringly between his eyes.

The ex-soldier's expression was bleak. Uncaring. Savage and primeval.

The gunman shook his head. 'No. Please.'

Garrett shook slightly as he fought for ascendancy. Fought for control.

Then, in three swift movements he stripped the pistol, throwing the barrel out of the window and dropping the frame and magazine to the floor.

'Alicia,' he said. His green eyes bored into her, flaying her. Exposing her.

'Yes,' she whispered.

'Let's go.'

She followed him meekly as he led her to the Land Rover, opened her door and strapped her seatbelt on.

He wasn't even breathing hard.

It took them four hours to drive home. During that time neither of them spoke. Garrett because he had nothing that he wanted to say. His job was done. He would take Alicia back to the main house and the laird would take care of things from thereon.

Alicia said nothing because she was already starting to yearn for another fix.

A needle to bring back the sunshine and drive back the oceans of her monstrous self-pity. A balm for her rampant selfishness. A band-aid to plaster over her self-evident stupidity.

Garrett's cell phone rang and he glanced at the incoming number and then picked it up. Eschewing the hands-free in order to have a private conversation that excluded Alicia.

'Petrus, my friend,' he greeted. 'Wassup?'

There was a pause filled only by the familiar echo and boom of the intercontinental satellite link and then the Zulu spoke.

'Hello, *Isosha*,' he said, using Garrett's Zulu nickname, The Soldier. 'I am sorry, but I have bad news. My youngest brother, Malusi. He is dead.'

Even across the thousands of intervening miles Garrett could hear Petrus' pain. The pain of losing a family member. The pain of losing a brother. The pain of losing a friend.

'I am so sorry. How did it happen?'

'He was murdered,' answered Petrus. 'Killed by savages.'

There was silence for a while. Garrett was not sure what to say.

'The body has already been laid out,' continued Petrus. 'The funeral is on Saturday.'

'I will be there,' said Garrett.

'Thank you,' answered Petrus. 'Thank you very much.'

Garrett ended the call and shifted down a gear. Eager to get home.

****

Well, there you go.

Thanks again – keep in touch.

Your friend in words

Craig